D1765092

# THE DUKE'S
# FIERY BRIDE

### DE WOLFE PACK
### THE SERIES

USA TODAY BESTSELLING AUTHOR

# HILDIE MCQUEEN

RECEIVED

Text copyright by the Author.

This work was made possible by special permission through the de Wolfe Pack Connected World publishing program and WolfeBane Publishing, a dba of Dragonblade Publishing. All characters, scenes, events, plots and related elements appearing in the original World of de Wolfe Pack connected series by Kathryn Le Veque Novels, Inc. remains the exclusive copyrighted and/or trademarked property of Kathryn Le Veque Novels, Inc., or the affiliates or licensors.

All characters created by the author of this novel remain the copyrighted property of the author.

# DE WOLFE PACK: THE SERIES

By Alexa Aston
*Rise of de Wolfe*

By Amanda Mariel
*Love's Legacy*

By Anna Markland
*Hungry Like de Wolfe*

By Autumn Sands
*Reflection of Love*

By Barbara Devlin
*Lone Wolfe: Heirs of Titus De Wolfe Book 1*
*The Big Bad De Wolfe: Heirs of Titus De Wolfe Book 2*
*Tall, Dark & De Wolfe: Heirs of Titus De Wolfe Book 3*

By Cathy MacRae
*The Saint*

By Christy English
*Dragon Fire*

By Hildie McQueen
*The Duke's Fiery Bride*

By Kathryn Le Veque
*River's End*

By Lana Williams
*Trusting the Wolfe*

By Laura Landon
*A Voice on the Wind*

By Leigh Lee
*Of Dreams and Desire*

By Mairi Norris
*Brabanter's Rose*

By Marlee Meyers
*The Fall of the Black Wolf*

By Mary Lancaster
*Vienna Wolfe*

By Meara Platt
*Nobody's Angel*
*Bhrodi's Angel*
*Kiss an Angel*

By Mia Pride
*The Lone Wolf's Lass*

By Ruth Kaufman
*My Enemy, My Love*

By Sarah Hegger
*Bad Wolfe on the Rise*

By Scarlett Cole
*Together Again*

By Victoria Vane
*Breton Wolfe Book 1*
*Ivar the Red Book 2*
*The Bastard of Brittany Book 3*

By Violetta Rand
*Never Cry de Wolfe*

# TABLE OF CONTENTS

# CHAPTER ONE

*Spring, 1274 AD*

*Castle Lasing, North Cumbria, England*

T HE ARROW WHIZZED past his head and imbedded itself into the tree. Gavin Mereworth, the recently appointed Duke of Selkirk, ducked low, pulled his sword and scanned the surrounding area for whoever the archer was. He was aware a title brought consequences. However, Gavin had not considered someone would try to kill him just days after being titled.

Shuffling and the crunching of branches were followed by a woman's curses and a soft groan. Whoever the female was, she seemed to be quite angry.

"Damn you, whoever you are. Come out so I can stab you properly." Once again leaves crunched and, finally, a young woman rushed toward him through the foliage.

Wearing a tunic, which was pulled up and tied around her waist, with a strap to display men's britches, the woman dressed quite strangely.

Gavin stood to his full height with his sword at the ready.

For only a second did her gaze flicker to the sword before moving to his face and then she huffed and rolled her green eyes.

"Only a fool wanders about these woods during a boar hunt. Do you have a death wish?"

The sound of hounds and loud voices nearby made her frown in the direction. "Now because of you, I won't find the wily beast." As if for emphasis, she lifted her bow and shook it at him. "I thought you were a boar."

Gavin regarded the woman. With her long, dark hair braided back, it made her large eyes, the color of fallen leaves, and petulant mouth easier to gaze upon. On her right cheek, a smearing of dirt tempted him to reach out and wipe it away. She was tall and slender. Even in her unique attire, there were no illusions of her not being female. She was astonishingly fetching.

"I am aware there is a boar hunt in progress," he began, measuring his words. "However, it is supposed to be limited to the other side of the stream."

Her gaze fell to the ground for an instant before

snapping back up to his. "So you say."

"I do say." He lifted his chin just a bit and peered down his nose at her. "Now kindly go on your way. I am searching for my injured hound."

Her change of countenance was immediate. Eyes rounded and her lips parted. "Injured? How?"

With an indignant huff, she motioned to his sword, palm up. "Did you cut the poor animal down? You seem enamored with your sword."

Gavin's lips thinned, he'd not realized that he had been holding the weapon up, still, and lowered it. With a droll look, he replied. "I heard a cry before he raced in this direction."

"I'll help you find him then." She fastened her bow onto a strap on her quiver and waited for him to sheathe his sword.

"You almost killed me. How do I know you don't plan to accost me once we are deeper into the woods?" Gavin walked in the direction he'd seen his hound go as she fell in step beside him.

A huff was her only reply.

Time passed slowly, each minute dragging by as they continued forward through the dense woods, not finding the dog. Gavin imagined the worst but managed to keep from showing despair in hopes they'd find his beloved companion.

"Shhh," the woman held up her hand. "I hear something."

Spotting the hound, Gavin rushed to where Lasitor lay under a thicket licking his right upper leg. The large dog let out a low whimper but at the same time wagged his tail upon spotting him.

"Come on, fellow. Let me pick you up. I'll try not to hurt you." Gavin coaxed the dog closer until he was finally able to wrap his arms around the animal to lift him.

It was a long walk back to where he'd tethered his horse and Gavin considered stopping to catch his breath and allow his aching arms to rest.

"Let me help." The woman held her arms out as his breathing had become labored from the weight of the heavy dog. They'd almost made it back to where they'd met, which meant it would still be quite a ways before reaching his horse.

Pride, however, kept him from accepting her assistance. "I can manage."

Lasitor eyed him as if knowing he stretched the truth. In all honesty, his arms burned from the dog's weight and his back had begun protesting a while earlier.

"Give me the damn dog." She stood before him arms outstretched. "If you drop him, he will get hurt worse."

After a long breath, he spoke through clenched teeth. "Very well, but my horse is not too far off now."

Once again, she rolled her eyes and it almost made him smile. Although it was obvious the dog was much too heavy, she managed well, allowing his arms time to recover.

"What is your name?" Gavin realized that, too worried about his dog, he'd not asked her as yet.

"Beatrice Preston," she stated primly. "Who are you?"

He'd yet to accept that his father had died so recently and passed the title of duke to him. However, he'd not shirk his responsibilities and soon would assume control of the lands and people.

"Gavin Mereworth, the lord is my uncle."

"Ah, so you're a high born then?" Her gaze moved over him as if measuring his status. "My condolences on the current passing of your Duke."

So she was not aware of whom exactly he was. The

idea of not having to assume any kind of persona at the moment allowed a needed respite. "Thank you."

"I hear there is a big feast planned by your relative, Lord Mereworth tomorrow. My father, brother and mother will be in attendance."

"Why not you?" He hoped to see her again. Something about her, the independence and lack of demureness, two things he'd never considered good attributes in a woman, took his interest now.

"I have better things to do than sit around minding my manners while my father attempts to find me a husband amongst the idiots in attendance."

His lips quivered. "I will be in attendance."

"You can take the dog now. I must be on my way." She unapologetically changed the subject.

Gavin took Lasitor, who whimpered at the jostling. Beatrice patted the dog's head and made cooing sounds. "There, there, you'll be well soon."

Gavin had already made up his mind; before he returned to home, he'd see Beatrice again. Sooner rather than later would be preferable as he was not yet aware how long he'd remain there. "Since you almost killed me and then called me an idiot, I do believe you owe me a dance Lady Beatrice."

Seeming to contemplate how to answer, pearly teeth sunk into her bottom lip. "It was a warning shot."

"If I'd moved but a bit forward, your warning would have fallen on dead ears."

"I didn't call everyone an idiot. My brother will be there. Although it is not his choice really since he is a guardsman for the lord."

"So, I await your presence tomorrow. I will inform my uncle to expect you."

Her shoulders fell and she eyed him for a moment before giving him a slow nod. Without another word, she turned and disappeared into the woods.

"I AM SURE you will shoulder the responsibilities that come with becoming a duke and bearing the title well young Gavin." His uncle's half-closed eyes regarded him as he spoke. "However, there is much you should be prepared for. Precautions need to be taken. More guards."

Gavin and his brother, Sinclair, the head of his guard, along with their other uncle and cousin surrounded a large table in the great room. Any guard who'd been in the room had been dispatched. Only trusted men remained guarding the doorway to allow the group privacy.

"I understand, Uncle. However, I do not believe it is necessary for you to send anyone back with me. I left the castle and people in the hands of the man father trusted the most. Torquil counseled him well for many years and will do the same for me. I have more than enough guardsmen."

As irritating as it all was, he'd known upon accepting his uncle's invitation, there would be testing and manipulation. If anyone resented the lands not being his, it was his uncle, Lord John Mereworth, who'd never been content to be second born. However, his bitterness had lightened upon being given a lordship of his own.

His other uncle, Alasdair, third born and without title, lived there on the family lands. With enough coin to never have to worry, he spent every living moment to instigate and annoy. Alasdair leaned forward and pointed at Gavin. "De Wolfe will test you. Mark my word on this."

Gavin had already reached out to Scott De Wolf and arranged for a meeting as his father's trusted friend had advised him. Torquil, although just a bit older than Gavin, was quite knowledgeable in family affairs. "I have it handled. Now, can we discuss the state of affairs with the Tarlington's?"

Upon mentioning his uncle's weak point, the lack of peace between him and the Tarlington's, a knight bent on destroying his uncle, John's nostrils flared. "Of course."

The discussion continued until the sun began to fall. Gavin was anxious to check on Lasitor. However, at this point, any indication on his part of caring for an animal would be seen as a weakness. Seeming to understand the direction of his thoughts as he continuously looked to the door, Sinclair leaned to his ear. "I will go see about the hound."

To the room, his brother announced his need to relieve himself and left.

That night, they would eat at the same table while keeping the conversation superficial and light.

William Tarlington, their sworn enemy, was wily and had, no doubt, bought an ear or two in their clan. Gavin was sure of it since they'd done the same.

SOMETIME LATER, THEY'D exhausted all on the subject of Tarlington. His uncle studied him as Gavin lifted a glass of whisky to his lips. "You are aware that as the new leader of your father's people, you must ensure the continuance of our lineage. I have fathered a babe here and there." He waved his hand as if children were inconsequential. "However, all are lasses."

His uncle, Alasdair, didn't comment on the fact he'd yet to produce any children. Gavin had his suspicions as to why, but kept them to himself.

"I will do so when the time is right. At this moment, my priority is to settle the people and see about preparations for the winter season. Marriage and fathering will come."

Alasdair pursed his lips and pinned him with wide eyes. "And if you were to die in the not so distant future? Who would carry your title?"

The title would end with him. Everyone knew it. If he were to be honest, he cared little about the damned title and would gladly give it and everything else up in exchange for his father to still be alive.

"Sinclair could petition for it."

"Unfortunately, my brother is correct. However, there is a chance it would not be passed to your brother." The lord studied him. "If you'd like, I can suggest a lass from within my lordship. We have plenty with families of good standing."

Unlike Gavin, who didn't reply, Alasdair leaned over his crossed legs and tapped his lips with a finger. "Do reveal your thoughts Brother on who you presume would be a good match for our nephew. I am very interested."

"It matters not," Gavin interjected. "I have no plans to marry in the foreseeable future. There is more pressing matters to attend to."

"Beatrice Preston would be my choice." His uncle paused for effect. "Her family, specifically her father and brother, would be a remarkable asset to me...us."

At the mention of the fiery lass he'd met earlier, Gavin couldn't help but be intrigued as to why his uncle considered her a suitable candidate for a wife. "I don't believe I know this family."

Alasdair nodded. "The family arrived just two years past. The brother was recruited to the guard for his brawn and abilities with the sword. The family, although wealthy, have claimed no alliance to a specific lord since arriving.

"You remind me of something, Brother," John said while he rubbed his chin. "Preston has yet to swear his fealty. The son, Oscar, a member of our guard, of course has, but not the patriarch."

Gavin was glad for the diversion from any marriage. However, it piqued his interest to learn something about Beatrice's family.

"I find it hard to believe you have allowed a head of a family not to do so, Uncle."

John looked to the doorway. "Tomorrow is soon enough to see to this matter, I suppose. They will be here for the feasting."

Both of his uncles, although younger than his father, had not aged well. The penchant for drinking too much ale and whisky every evening would be Gavin's guess. How unfair it was that his father, the most virile of the three, had fallen first. His death came after a slight injury suffered during sword practice had festered. The wound sent him into a deathlike sleep from which his strong, virile father never woke.

Alasdair uncrossed his too-thin legs and blew out a breath. "I am not looking forward to the celebration. Not so soon after losing our brother. I find it in bad taste."

Every head turned to him with incredulous expressions. Alasdair loved any occasion for feasting and drinking. Undaunted, his uncle continued. "To think. We are in mourning. We should have put the visitors off for at least a fortnight."

"It's too late and you know it." John stood, signaling the end to their talk. "I must prepare for last meal." His shrewd gaze slid to Gavin. "The topic of your marriage remains unfinished. We shall speak of it at length before you depart."

# CHAPTER TWO

WHILE A LARGE boar was paraded, the men in the lucky hunting party made annoying gestures toward Beatrice and her hunting group as people gathered to congratulate them.

"Where'd you go off to?" Her brother gave her an annoyed look, forehead creasing as his brows lowered. "You were supposed to help keep the beast on our side of the stream."

Beatrice looked past her brother at the men who were now doing some sort of dance. She could only describe it as obscene. "I helped a man find his wounded dog."

At once, her brother's full attention was hers. "Who?"

"Shouldn't you see about what the men are doing? If they begin removing clothing, I will round up the women and leave."

The man she'd met in the woods was tall with a

broad chest and wide shoulders. However, Gavin Mereworth would appear slight beside her bear of a twin brother, Oscar.

With a square jaw, thick, shoulder-length tresses and intense, light brown eyes, Oscar attracted many a woman's attention. And he rarely turned any away, garnering his rogue status amongst the villagers. When Oscar was about, fathers kept their daughters of age safely locked away once noting his presence.

However, she supposed, none would deny the warrior if he asked for any lass' hand. Not that Oscar was about to give up the plunder and settle any time soon.

"I don't recall the man's name. A friend or relative of the Lord's," Beatrice lied. "His hound was injured, we found it."

Oscar narrowed his eyes and leaned forward to study her face. "You didn't let that sharp tongue of yours loose, I hope."

"Shouldn't you be more worried about my virtue or perhaps that I could have been accosted?" Beatrice placed her fisted hands on both hips. "You are not a caring brother."

"Ha!" Oscar's bark of laughter made others turn to look. "I know you much better than that. Given you didn't answer my question, I am prepared to make amends for whatever it is you did."

Beatrice searched her mind thinking back to what she'd said. "Other than stating the men in attendance at the feast were idiots, I was too worried about the hound to insult him further."

"What did he say?" That Oscar could speak so clearly though clenched teeth and barely-moving lips had always astonished her. "Did he ask anything of you?"

It was her turn to press her lips together. "That I come tomorrow night." Beatrice mumbled the reply, leaving out the part of him asking for a dance. No matter how loyal Oscar was to Lord Mereworth, he would never allow any male to treat her badly. "That's all."

"Then you will go."

"I will not." She turned on her heel only to be flung back around so hard that she lost her balance. She grabbed Oscar's hair to keep from falling.

He yelped.

She lost her grip and fell.

Village children who'd been watching began circling her, laughing and pointing.

"You will," Oscar growled and stalked away.

Beatrice looked to the leader of the chanting circle.

"If you don't leave me be, you little beastie, I will toss you in the fire."

The child screamed and ran off crying, the others on his heels.

DEEP IN THOUGHT, Beatrice entered her home through the kitchen door. After traipsing in the woods, neither she nor Oscar was allowed through the front door.

The aroma of the evening meal made her stomach grumble. A reminder she'd not eaten since early that morning.

Meaghan, the cook, gave her a once over and pointed to a side door. "Go on inside there and remove those horrible rags. I will fetch water."

"Can I have a piece of bread?" She eyed the covered basket on the side table.

Without having to look, Beatrice knew the answer when Meaghan focused on her grimy hands. "No you may not."

Childish as it was, Beatrice wanted to cry. "I am so hungry."

"A proper young woman does not spend her day like a wildling in the woods, but at home. You would have had tea and an afternoon repast with your mother had you been home. Therefore, I have a hard time feeling sorry for you." Meaghan neared and pushed her to the bathing room. "Go on now. I haven't all day."

Beatrice undressed and loosed her hair. She gathered up a bucket of water and poured the cold water over her head. Shivering while she scrubbed, she was glad when Meaghan brought hot water to mix in with the next bucket.

Perhaps Meaghan was right. If she desired to marry and settle, it would not do to continue in her ways. As she washed her hair, Beatrice wondered if Gavin Mereworth was married.

"YOU WILL ATTEND the gathering." Her father gave Beatrice a pointed look while holding his speared meat halfway to his mouth.

Other than wishing the meat would fall and splash juices over his tunic, Beatrice had little recourse but to nod. "I don't see why everyone is suddenly so interested in my attendance at the feast. It used to be you urged me to stay home."

The exchange of looks between her parents sent a tingle down her spine. This time her mother spoke, a soft smile on her lips. "Beatrice, I worry about your penchant for hunting and lack of interest in womanly duties. We have been much too lenient. We must ensure you learn to perform properly in society, so you can marry well."

"Marry?" Beatrice's mouth fell open. "I don't wish to marry. Not yet anyway."

Oscar huffed. "Now you see? There is a problem with a woman her age not wanting to marry. She must be settled."

*Settled?* Beatrice straightened, her food forgotten. "I am not a sheep to be auctioned off."

There was a beat of silence. Her mother slid a pointed look at her father. Beatrice had a soft spot for her strong, quiet father. However, in instances like this, he had the power to make her quake. Although a fair and often too-lenient parent, when his mind was made up on something, he made his point quite clear.

He pointed his fork in her direction. "You will go to the gathering. You will comport yourself like a lady and I will ensure it is known you are ready to marry."

There was no need for him to ask if she understood. The message was clear. Her days of living at home were coming to an end. How she wished at that point to be ten years of age so crying and dashing to her bed would not be seen as weak. Instead, she let out a shaky breath before glaring at Oscar.

The oaf continued eating without a worry. "I think Oscar should settle as well. Bethany Blankenship confessed to me about having laid with him and fearing the possibility of consequences." Her triumphant look was met with her brother's food plopping from his open mouth to the table.

"I never bedded that wench." Oscar's eyes moved side to side as the scoundrel, no doubt, racked his brain to recall if the statement was true.

"If you did and her father finds out, you will be held responsible," their mother stated. "And I agree with Beatrice. The both of you are old enough to settle with families of your own."

A sharp kick made Beatrice flinch. When she returned it, she missed and her father grunted.

Oscar smirked only to sober when their father slammed his hands on the tabletop. "May we finish this meal in peace?"

"I apologize, Father," Beatrice said, eyes downcast as she leaned forward and pinched Oscar's leg as hard as she could, ensuring her nails sunk into his flesh.

Her brother grimaced and moved his leg away.

# CHAPTER THREE

G AVIN STROLLED INTO his brother's chamber without knocking only to stop at the sight of his brother's naked arse.

Unable to stop, as Sinclair seemed to be at the point of culmination, his brother chose to ignore his presence.

Allowing him privacy, Gavin stalked past the bed to the window only to be stopped when a hand reached out and grabbed his. A second wench lay beside the couple. Her passion-drunk gaze met his and she licked her lips. "Join us."

A grunt followed by a loud groan signaled Sinclair's release just as the woman beneath him cried out.

Gavin pulled his hand away slowly. "I don't join my brother in bedsport. The sight of him naked chases away any arousal on my part."

From the window, lights in the near distance could be seen. The village folks had settled for the night.

There were only a few people still up and about surrounding the large bonfire in the square. The boar hunt must have brought a good-sized prize.

"Why are you in here?" Sinclair growled more than asked. "As you can see, I'm preoccupied. I'm not in the mood for conversation."

Not bothering to turn around lest he see more of his brother's nude form, Gavin kept his gaze outward. "Uncle John. What am I missing?"

A woman moaned and Gavin chuckled. He should leave, as Sinclair was known to continue bedsport well into the night. However, the niggling in the back of his mind would not allow Gavin sleep. "Why do I feel as if I'm a pawn in a game between both uncles?"

Sounds of flesh against flesh became louder until the second woman's cry rang out. Moments later there was shuffling of clothing and whispered promises before the wenches left, both sending glares in Gavin's direction at his ruining their chance at sleeping in a plush bed with what he was sure they considered a very handsome man.

"Do you really not see it?" Sinclair sat in the bed, the bedding about his waist, sloppily. "Tis clear as day. They plot to marry you into a family with close ties to them, so that through your wife, they can manipulate you."

Gavin gave his brother a droll look. "I know that. But to what means? Neither uncle can aspire to the title. Beside, you are next in line to receive it if your petition is accepted."

"Perhaps they plan to poison me and, once you are alone, kill you." With a shrug, Sinclair reached to the table beside the bed and poured whisky, not bothering to offer him any. Although Gavin enjoyed the taste of it from time to time, he focused on always maintaining a clear mind.

Sinclair took a drink and studied him. "Although you are correct, if anything, they should not want you to marry and produce an heir. Perhaps we are overthinking it. We are well aware of Uncle Alasdair's penchant for drama and games. Mayhap that is all they seek out of this, some sort of game to enjoy."

Although he wasn't convinced, Gavin could not think of any plan that would benefit either uncle if he married.

"Have we become so hardened, that we look for bad in everything? Of all people, we should be able to trust our family."

Sinclair shook his head. "I don't know. Years of war and our father's recent death have affected our judgment. With the death of a powerful man, such as our father, there are always challenges to the seat."

"True. However, Uncle John's lord ship here is large and he seems content enough."

"For some people, the more power the better."

A distant look on his face, Sinclair sighed. "I miss him. He'd know exactly what to do. Father wouldn't have stood like you do now, but would have instantly dismissed the women so we could speak."

Gavin smiled. "True. I can see it now. He'd keep an eye on them the entire time, enjoying the view, but pretending not to."

A bark of laughter escaped his brother and Sinclair shook his head. "Remember the time he caught the maid, Gertrude, in your chambers and watched her get dressed not knowing mother was standing in the doorway behind him?"

"Ah, yes," Gavin laughed. "Mother made him sleep in the great room for several nights."

Gavin ignored the pang in his chest. "We must remain at least another week. Perhaps if something is amiss, we can figure it out by then."

The brothers looked at the fire in the hearth, both in thought. Finally, Gavin spoke again. "I met her. The lass Uncle John suggested I marry."

"Lass? What lass?"

"Beatrice Preston. She was part of the boar hunt today when I searched for Lasitor."

"And?" Sinclair leaned forward, his eyes locked to Gavin's face. "What happened?"

Although Sinclair could be a gentleman, most of the time he'd rather offend a woman with a suggestion of a tup in the shade than speaking of inconsequential things. "Did you..."

"I was searching for Lasitor. I did nothing more than allow her to walk with me."

"How enchanting." Sinclair's voice dripped with sarcasm.

Gavin ignored his comment. "She's a good archer. Seems to like animals."

"Enough to kill them? What did she look like? Are her breasts full or small?"

Considering he'd spent a couple hours in her company, Gavin had the time to memorize everything about her. From the loose tendrils framing her face, large green eyes, pouty lips and well-formed figure.

"She is quite fiery."

Gavin's flat gaze met Sinclair's. "So, homely then." He shrugged. "Don't marry her. If she is not attractive now, imagine what she'll look like in a few years." His brother shuddered.

It was impossible not to laugh at the shallowness. Gavin hit his brother on the shoulder. "Good night, Brother. Should I send the wenches back to you?"

Sinclair studied the empty, rumpled bed. "I don't know. I think not. I must rest so I can be clear of head and able to delve further into what we spoke of."

Satisfied that regardless of Sinclair's seeming lack of care, his brother would, indeed, investigate further. As second born, Sinclair had more freedoms. He was seen as a shallow woman chaser and that always played well for him. Those that knew his younger brother well recognized that he possessed a keen mind and intelligence much greater than most.

"Thank you."

"No need." Sinclair pushed the bedding off. "Now let me be."

"Ugh, gladly," Gavin turned away.

LATER, IN HIS own bed, Gavin considered it strange

he'd not divulged how lovely Beatrice was to his brother. No doubt, upon learning of the beautiful lass, Sinclair would have been anxious to meet her. As charming as his brother was, it was doubtful that even the fiery lass could be indifferent.

Turning to lay on his stomach, Gavin punched at the pillows and blew out a breath. The next eve would be most interesting, indeed.

VISITORS BEGAN ARRIVING early the next day. Those that could not be housed indoors pitched tents and settled into the huge courtyard. Already, people from surrounding villages had settled on the lands surrounding the castle as the festivities were always eventful and great feasts were prepared and shared with everyone in attendance.

Alasdair sat at the high board next to Gavin, his eyes scanning the room searching the faces. Nostrils flared and eyes narrowed he turned to Gavin. "Do you know the men at the table next to the hearth?"

Four men sat, two on each side of the table on the benches, tearing bread from loaves and eating with gusto. By their dirty, bearded faces and soiled tunics, it was hard to tell if they'd traveled far and just arrived or were roaming men looking for work.

"No, I do not. However, they seem to know people here."

"Aye. I notice that now." His uncle turned to look at his brother. "It is probably John's doing. Inviting people from every corner of neighboring lands."

"Are the Tarlington's expected to cause problems?"

"No," Alasdair exclaimed. "The scouts claim there is no movement from the north. However, if they did show their faces, it would make this a memorable event, indeed." His eyes shined and his lips curved. "Someone should have slipped word to them."

Gavin wondered how anyone could stand being around Alasdair for more than a few moments. It was like speaking to a child, at times. Unfortunately, his uncle's penchant for scheming was usually quite elevated. "I believe they are aware."

His uncle's expression became hooded. "Of course they are."

Once again, apprehension came and Gavin looked across the room for Sinclair, who'd refused to sit at the high board. His brother ate with the guard and looked to be in deep conversation with a tall, muscular man. Hopefully, he was gleaning information that would prove useful.

# CHAPTER FOUR

B EATRICE ENSURED TO keep her shoulders back and back rigid as they proceeded into the castle's interior. The line of people waiting to greet the lord and family was long. Thankfully, she and her parents had arrived early and were close to the high board. They would soon greet the lord and be able to sit at the table. She scanned the room for her brother and found him in conversation with a man she didn't recognize.

Whatever they spoke of seemed to draw them to lean in close in order to hear over the din of the voices in the room.

From the well-made tunic, the man was of means, which meant he was probably a relative of the lord. Although his wavy hair reminded her of Gavin Mereworth, it was not he.

Her mother nudged her forward. Beatrice glanced up to the high board just in time to meet the gaze of none other than the man she'd just been thinking about.

The person in front of him bowed and began to speak. Gavin lowered his head to her in a subtle nod just as his attention was taken by the man before him.

Lord Mereworth seemed to be making some sort of elaborate introduction and, by the reactions of the people, Beatrice wondered what was being said.

"You would think a noble is here by the way the Dugan's just shoved their daughter to stand before the high board," Beatrice mumbled, only to be elbowed by her mother.

"Hush, they will hear you."

Her mother's elbow had hit its mark. Her rib protested and Beatrice covered the affected area with both hands. "That hurt."

She was yanked forward by her father and made to stand between her parents as he stated their names to the lord and thanked him for the hospitality.

There was a strange exchange between Lord Mereworth and his brother, Alasdair, a man with a flair for the dramatic. Beatrice had always found his actions amusing.

"I introduce to you my nephew, Gavin Mereworth, Lord of Hardigg and newly appointed Duke of

Selkirk." The Lord seemed winded by the long title.

Beatrice's wide eyes were met by the duke's flat ones and her mother hissed in her ear. "Close your mouth."

Her father caught Lord Mereworth's attention. "I was led to believe you had two nephews visiting."

Lord Mereworth motioned to the back of the room. "My other nephew, Sinclair, has not deemed it necessary to join us and is, instead, in the back of the room with the guards. He speaks to your son now."

"He is a member of my guard, Uncle. Therefore, he feels more at ease in their company," Gavin said to the lord.

Lord Mereworth didn't reply. Instead, his keen eyes locked on Beatrice before speaking to her father. "Is the lass betrothed as yet?"

Not moving her head, Beatrice slid her gaze to her father.

"Not as yet, Lord. However, we are seeking a match for her."

Her stomach sank and her cheeks burned with mortification as Gavin's attention remained riveted on her. There were many people waiting to be introduced. Surely, there was a better time to discuss all of this.

"It occurs to me," Alasdair began, "your family has yet to become a true member of our Lordship's. Perhaps by marriage we can become more united."

What exactly was happening, Beatrice wasn't sure. She let out an impatient huff and turned to see her brother's attention was toward the front of the room. So, it seemed, was all of the nearby people's.

"Very true," her father proclaimed. "I am not sworn to you as of yet Lord. However, my son has given not just his oath but his sword as well to ye."

Lord Mereworth nodded. However, Alasdair was not to be silenced. "Marriage, perhaps of your son to the lord's daughter, Mara, or even Anne. She is of age is she not?" he asked his brother, who seemed bored with the conversation, by his sigh.

"We shall discuss this further." Lord Mereworth gave Gavin a pointed look. "My own nephews are both without wives, which is fine for the young Sinclair. However, His Grace must find a wife soon."

His Grace looked to his uncle with lowered brows. "Uncle, we should allow them to find their place. The food comes now."

Beatrice let out a sigh of relief and gladly allowed her mother to guide her away. She turned to the glares of every woman in the near vicinity. Obviously, she'd just made enemies of the hopefuls to be the duke's wife.

After spending time with him earlier, it was obvious to her the man was no closer to marriage than she was. If anything, by the way he doted on his dog and had constantly scanned the room, she wondered if perhaps his assignation was more toward his own sex.

His uncle, Alasdair, after all, was well known to share his bed with several men. One of her own male acquaintances had admitted to being asked to join the lord's brother for bedsport. She'd laughed at his mortification. He'd promptly responded by rushing to the pub and going up the stairs with two wenches, probably to prove more to himself than anyone else of his preference. Beatrice couldn't help but find humor in the entire situation as her friend prided himself in being a rake.

In the great room, the constant conversation mingled with cups being raised and music playing loudly. Surprisingly, Beatrice found the evening to be quite entertaining.

She walked about the room with her friend Elizabeth, who hoped to get Oscar's attention. Beatrice tried to convince her friend to walk up to her brother and start a conversation, but Elizabeth insisted it would be unbecoming.

So now, they made a second circle. Beatrice enjoyed the stroll since she could eavesdrop on conversations and return glares to the women whose gazes followed her.

"I don't believe we've been formally introduced." The handsome man who'd been talking to her brother blocked their path. "I am Sinclair Mereworth, the lord's nephew."

Elizabeth blinked, her eyes rounded, while Beatrice bent her head. "I am Beatrice and this is my friend, Elizabeth."

The duke's brother was dashing. A lock fell over his brow, giving him a roguish air as he took each of their hands and pressed his lips to the knuckles in a very formal fashion.

"Oh my." Elizabeth was breathless, making Beatrice wonder if she'd faint.

Beatrice stood straighter and looked to the handsome man. "Would you care to join us as we parade around the room?"

"May I ask why you find the need to do so?" he

asked. "Every eye is on you. If you are not aware, ladies, you are the most beautiful woman here."

It wouldn't do to laugh out loud at the duke's brother. So, instead, she looked to where Gavin had been seated, only to find the spot empty.

"Brother, I see you've met my friend, Beatrice Preston." When his possessive hand took her elbow, Beatrice looked to the doorway and a thought crossed her mind. If she made a dash for it, would she reach a horse and escape before either her brother or father caught up to her?

"Brothers?" Beatrice looked from one to the other, noticing the resemblance upon closer inspection. Her lips curved at the challenge between the men. It never ceased to amaze her how often the male species acted more like beasts of the wild than humans, no matter their station.

"I have a brother as well. Oscar is a guard for our lord." She looked toward Oscar who poured ale down his throat as if putting out a fire. Not exactly the intimidating effect she hoped for.

Sinclair and Gavin never broke eye contact. However, the younger of the two did respond. "I've met him."

None too gently, Beatrice pulled her arm free of Gavin's grasp. "I do believe mother calls us, Elizabeth." She tugged her dazed friend away toward where her parents, who'd been smiling at seeing her speaking to the brothers. The smiles were replaced with frowns of displeasure at her abrupt disentanglement. No matter, she'd not be pushed into throwing herself at a man just for them to be rid of her.

Her mother leaned into her ear as soon as she sat. "Did one of them ask you for a walk in the garden?"

"No, Mother, they were too busy staring at each other."

"Why did you walk away then? Go back. Both seemed very interested. The eldest is a *duke.*" Her mother emphasized the last word, in case she'd forgotten Gavin's title.

Lips curving at her poor mother's annoyance, she pressed a kiss to the woman's jaw. "Why would a duke marry a village girl, Mother? Let us be realistic. Even the brother would be lowering himself to marry me."

Her mother pinched her arm. "Don't be daft, girl. Our family is of good standing." Beatrice's arm stung from the hard pinch. "Get up and go back now."

"Ow." Rubbing her upper arm, Beatrice jumped to

her feet and rushed away to her brother, who let out a loud burp. "It's a wonder he's not married," Beatrice mumbled to Elizabeth who'd also been dispatched by her mother.

Elizabeth let out a dreamy sigh. "He is most handsome."

"He is a nasty boor." Beatrice softened when Oscar smiled at her. "However, he is loveable." She tugged her suddenly reluctant friend to where Oscar sat.

"Brother, I must speak to you. It is important."

Oscar looked to her, moved his eyes to Elizabeth and then allowed his gaze to linger on his tankard. "Now?"

"Yes, now." Beatrice gripped Elizabeth's arm as her friend attempted to move away. The poor girl trembled at being so close to her oblivious brother.

"Very well." He stood, hesitated and then lifted his cup. "What is it?"

"Come." Beatrice used her free hand to tug at his tunic.

They made their way to the back of the room near a small alcove. "Our parents expect me to make a fool of myself and fawn over the duke and his brother. Would you please ensure the two don't come near me again?"

"Why would I do that?" Oscar looked across the room to where the brothers remained. People now surrounded them. Parents shoved their flushed-faced daughters before the seemingly overwhelmed duo.

Oscar chucked. "I don't believe you have to worry about them. Every lass will be paraded before them for the rest of the evening." He pointed to where musicians set up to play for the upcoming dance. "Look."

"Entertain Elizabeth for a moment. I'll return shortly."

Oscar looked to her friend as if noticing her for the first time. Beatrice dashed away, ignoring Elizabeth's loud gasp.

At the guards' table, the men pretended not to notice as she neared. Afraid of her beast of a brother and her contrary disposition, most kept a distance whenever she was about. Beatrice searched the faces until finding Finlay, a slender young archer she'd been a friend with since childhood.

Her friend, who'd, traveled with her family when coming to Cumbria as a squire to her father, lifted a brow in question but stood at her pointed look. Despite the fact he was in love with a village girl, he puffed out his chest and walked to Beatrice. "Beatrice, whatever could possibly bother you on this fair day?"

Sarcasm dripped from every word and Beatrice scowled. "Am I that unpleasant that my being annoyed doesn't worry you in the least?"

Finlay remained quiet, so Beatrice hit his arm. "Will you dance with me?"

"The music has not yet started." He searched the room. "Whose attention are you attempting to get?"

Beatrice huffed. "Not attention, but the opposite. My parents are attempting to marry me off and I do not wish to be. Not yet. I want to choose my future husband."

Finlay's eyes grew round.

"Are you listening to me? I refuse to make a fool out of myself by fawning over that fancy duke and his brother. It's obvious they are untamed rakes."

Letting out a long breath, Finlay looked up to the ceiling.

"Am I to presume I wasted my time coming to ensure you repay your promise of a dance?" The smoothness in Gavin's deep voice, so different from any she'd heard fell over her. Unfortunately, due to what she'd just spoken, the effect was more like cold water than anything else.

The search for an appropriate response came up empty. Instead, Beatrice turned and smiled at him. "It is not nice to eavesdrop on conversations Your Grace. Sometimes, one hears things not meant for one's ears."

"Obviously." His dark gaze was flat, but the corners of his pressed-together lips curved. "However, Miss Preston, rakes don't always behave properly."

Hoping to get support, she turned, only to find Finlay had returned to his seat and kept his head down. Not exactly a true friend, then, to abandon one during times of trouble.

"Are you enjoying your coming out party?" She lifted her nose and scanned the room hoping annoyed parents would rush over and shove her out of the way in order to garner the duke's attention. It wasn't that she found him unappealing, quite the opposite. If Beatrice was to be honest, he was exactly the type of man she'd always dreamed of marrying.

Handsome, sensual, tall, broad-shouldered, with silky tresses that fell to his shoulders and a roguish smile that made her stomach tumble. It had not been unnoticed by her that his legs and arms were well formed, his backside taut from horseback riding. Yes, the man who stood before her was not just every woman's dream, but hers as well.

"Should I be afraid?" he drawled. "You are looking at me like a woman starved."

Her eyes rounded before she could make herself look away. "I am quite hungry. I was just thinking of the boar meat from the hunt. It was quite succulent."

The music started and the duke took her arm. "Your mother tells me you love walks about the garden. How about some fresh air before we dance?"

It was hard not to grin at noticing her mother's wide smile directed at her and every single glare from the other women present as Gavin walked her toward an open doorway. When they passed a table of young women who stared at her companion, Beatrice stopped and looked up at him. "If you're in need of fresh air, any of the women behind me would gladly accompany you."

None too gently, he guided her by the elbow until outside. They descended the stairs in silence to the lord's beautiful gardens. Despite the sudden thumping of her heart at being alone with the duke, Beatrice had to admire the beauty surrounding her. Fragrant blooms swayed in the gentle breeze as their perfumes intermingled in the air. Lady Mereworth obviously knew which flowers to plant where, as every plant flourished.

Next to short hedges, benches were scattered here and there seemingly without thought or pattern. However upon closer inspection it was obvious that each would garner a quiet private spot to talk. Exactly the place Beatrice would avoid this night at all costs. She continued past a bench, pretending the flowers took all her attention.

In truth, the man next to her took every single ounce of concentration to ignore. He let out a long breath and stopped walking. "It's a lovely night, is it not?"

Gavin, the rake, looked down. He didn't meet her gaze but instead, studied her cleavage. Damn the cut of the dress her mother insisted she wear.

On her mother, the neckline was acceptable. Since Beatrice's breasts were quite larger, they practically over spilled. "It's my mother's dress. She insisted I wear it. I see the bait works. However, as you may suspect, I am not interested in any romantic notions."

"It's a shame." He smiled and her legs wavered. Perhaps the bench would have been a better idea than standing, especially when he moved closer. "You're a beauty. I am shocked that you are not surrounded by admirers."

Beatrice turned to gaze past his shoulder. "Yes, well, you do not have a problem with that."

"Beatrice?" Something about the way he pronounced her name made her breathing hitch. How did he do it? To gain such a reaction from just speaking one word was new to her.

"Yes?"

About to insist they return inside as the music now wafted in the air, she turned her attention back to him. Gavin's mouth covered hers. The kiss was soft yet not gentle. Demanding, but at the same time allowing her to respond as he kept his body apart from hers.

Her eyelids fluttered shut and she didn't quite allow the kiss. Instead, it lingered because of her inability to move away. Sensations of warmth and excitement weaved around her from head to toe until everything else disappeared. In the moment his lips moved over her mouth, all that existed was Gavin.

It would be their only kiss, Beatrice decided, and enjoy it she would. Afraid he'd move away, she took his shoulders and parted her lips. Not because she was experienced, but because it seemed the natural thing to do. To taste more of him, to take him deeper.

Gavin's tongue pushed past her teeth to tangle with hers. He then deepened the kiss by pulling her against him. Leaning her face to the side, his mouth continued to ravage her until the kiss made every inch of her hum with pleasure.

The sense of falling brought her arms around his neck and Beatrice clung to Gavin, not quite sure how to stop. It had to end. It was enough.

His lips traveled down her jawline and Gavin's teeth sunk into her neck. It wasn't hard enough to be painful. No, it was not what she would describe as physical pain, but there was an ache.

The sensation shocked her back to reality.

"Ah!" Beatrice pushed away. Her breathing hitched as she struggled to get a full breath.

It helped, somewhat, to see he did the same, his chest expanding and lowering as he held her by the arms. Not so much to control, but because she swayed.

"Are you able to stand without assistance?"

Beatrice pushed his hands away. "Of course."

When her knees threatened to give way, he guided her to the bench.

"I have to say, I must sit for a bit, too."

With his arms across his lap, as if to cover up, Gavin leaned forward and let out several breaths. "I cannot go inside for a few moments. Neither of us can. I would embarrass us."

"Why would I be embarrassed? What is wrong with you? Are you in pain?" The heat between her legs was becoming manageable. Mostly due to his continuous huffs and strange demeanor.

Finally, Gavin seemed to feel better as he straightened and studied her for a moment. "Do you not know about a man's aroused state? It can be quite obvious."

Beatrice looked to anywhere but between his legs. "Oh. I suppose so." Feeling foolish, she stood. "I best go inside. I suppose our…kiss makes up for the dance then."

"No it does not." His gaze traveled up her body and Beatrice almost fidgeted, but kept still. "As a matter of fact, we should dance all night."

"I am not interested in you, sir." Beatrice placed her fisted hands on her hips. "As a matter of fact, I don't understand why you insist on it. Your future potential for a wife could be inside while you dally about out here with me."

Gavin stood, his broad body blocking her view of

the entrance. "You do not fool me. You can barely keep your eyes from me and you are not hard to see through."

The lack of breathing properly had obviously weakened the man's ability to make any sense. She turned her eyes up to the starlit sky then to the bushes, anything to keep from looking directly at him. It was not easy.

He continued to stare at her as if waiting for a reply, so she obliged. "Whatever are you talking about?"

"You are fearless, yet vulnerable. Although there is an air of lack of caring, I saw the way you helped your friend to spend time with your brother. Your friend, the archer, is proud of you. Your parents know your worth. The women in the room are not just envious of your beauty, but of your confidence and independence."

For the first time since she could remember, Beatrice could not think of what to say. The statement was so rich, so different than anything that anyone had ever said about and to her.

Seeming to understand she was without words, the duke led her back to the great room. Moments later, she found herself dancing with the most handsome man in the room.

# CHAPTER FIVE

G AVIN WASN'T AT all surprised to find Beatrice had disappeared halfway through the night. The woman was as puzzling as she was enticing. He suffered yet another dance with a woman who kept stepping on his feet since she concentrated too much on his face. "I apologize. I do not know what has gotten into me. I am usually a good dancer."

Thankfully, the song ended and he could escort the now pouting woman back to where she'd been sitting. "I am so winded. Fresh air would be nice." She batted her eyelashes at him.

"Ah, my uncle calls," Gavin exclaimed and dashed away.

Alasdair peered down his nose at the people gathered then over to the dancers. "I expected more entertainment than just your escapade with the feisty girl, Beatrice."

Gavin pressed his lips to keep from laughing.

"What about the red-haired guardsman? I caught him slipping out a side door with someone unexpected in tow."

Straightening, Alasdair searched the room. "Pray tell, who did he leave with?"

Settling into the chair next to his uncle, Gavin motioned a nearby serving woman for ale. "I find it more amusing to allow you the opportunity to figure it out for yourself, Uncle."

Although Alasdair scowled, his eager gaze continued searching the room until widening. "Mullen's wife?" The corners of his lips lifted as he leaned forward, chin resting on his right hand. "If Mullen catches wind of this, the man will not be subtle."

It mattered not to Gavin what happened, but what he hoped was to allow Alasdair to become distracted enough to not guard his words. "Uncle, do you honestly feel I should marry soon?"

Mullen stood and trekked across the room toward the garden doors. Alasdair waved a dismissive hand to Gavin. "You should marry. Our family must keep the title."

"If I were to meet with misfortune, there is always Sinclair and if we are both overcome and killed, you or

Uncle John would take it."

Alasdair tracked Mullen as the older man now headed to the guards' table. "John will not have a male heir. He and Alice no longer share a bed. I won't marry. Even if I were to…" He stopped speaking as Mullen's wife meandered from the back of the room. The red-haired guard was not with her.

Mullen hurried to her and seemed to be questioning his wife.

"I wonder if the guard is wise enough to stay absent?" Alasdair exclaimed with exaggerated glee.

Gavin rolled his eyes. "I have plenty of time then. No hurry."

When the couple went to sit, not seeming either angry or happy for that matter, Alasdair finally turned his attention back to Gavin.

"The Duke of Aldorf has petitioned to the crown for your title to be given to his own brother. The brother, you know, has tried to kill him several times. He grows tired of sleeping with an open eye, I suppose. With enough coin, his brother can buy even the duke's closest guards to slit his throat."

The entire business of titles and such was of little importance to Gavin. Not worth it in his opinion.

However, the title was a matter of much pride within the family since it had been awarded to Gavin's grandfather for bravery.

"Why didn't you tell me?"

"There is no specific reason, dear boy. We believe the threat is not strong. Not yet. However, once you sire a male heir, the duke will lose ground. Until you sire a boy child, one of his strongest weapons is the lack of a new direct heir after you."

Rage surged and Gavin clenched the tankard. "Father has only been dead a few weeks."

A sigh escaped Alasdair and his brows lowered. "I miss my brother dearly. If anything, I expected him to live the longest. I understand you mourn Gavin. However, your duties as Lord and titled Duke of Selkirk come first. You must produce an heir with haste."

In essence, whether he loved the woman he married or not mattered little. What was important was to marry and to produce a male child. The woman would have to be prepared to have a second child in short order if the first was not a male child. Gavin scanned the room. Not seeing anything, his mind clouded. "When did you plan to tell me all this?"

"The true reason for this gathering. The reason every family brings lasses from near and far is because word has been spread. You will be choosing a wife soon."

Now he understood the reference by Beatrice to it being his "coming out party."

"Uncle. You should have told me upon my arrival. Why all the secrecy?"

Finally, Alasdair looked to his brother. "He will be cross upon learning I've told you all this. We know you. You are so much like him. Like your father. You will not be forced into anything. Your father requested we help you marry as soon as he passed. He also told us you would resist it."

Alasdair lifted a shoulder. "I can't keep secrets."

"My father planned this?"

"No. The gathering was my idea. Oh look." The red-haired guard entered and looked around the room until finding Mullen's wife. The woman fidgeted, refusing to make eye contact. Mullen jumped to his feet and rushed to where the guard stood.

"Now, it's about to get interesting," Alasdair exclaimed.

Gavin searched out Beatrice's brother. The large

male remained at the guards' table. He stood and made his way to intercede between the guard and Mullen.

The night was about to become interesting, indeed.

⟫⟫⟫⟪⟪⟪

"No. I don't believe you." Beatrice collapsed into the cushions of the chair she sat upon. "He asked for us to be married?"

Her mother practically floated across the floor. "Aye, he did. Most formally. He had Oscar present his request to your father."

Of course, her mother failed to see that neither she nor Beatrice were included in the decision. "I don't want to marry him. I'll have to live far away."

"It's not that far," her father grumbled and frowned at her. "The Lord has requested we return tomorrow for the exchange of vows."

"Tomorrow!" Beatrice jumped to her feet. "No. I refuse." She looked to Oscar for help, her spirits boosted when he came to stand beside her.

"Why can't we ask for a fortnight?" her brother interceded. "Beatrice needs time to grow used to the idea. I can take her to his castle when the time is right."

"She will marry and be bedded tomorrow and that

is final. The Lord already questions our fealty. This will prove our loyalty to him and ensure your mother and I have a place to grow old without fear of being sent away on a whim." Her father refused to listen to anything more. Instead, he pointed at them both. "Oscar, you can travel with your sister to Hardigg Castle. Vow loyalty and join His Grace's guard if you wish. But the marriage will happen."

This time, it was her mother who looked stricken. One hand over her mouth, her wide eyes looked to her husband. "Both...both my children...are to leave?"

"Enough." Although the command was quiet, there was no room for argument.

Beatrice's father left the room, her mother tagging behind, no doubt, to try to talk their father out of sending Oscar away. Although Beatrice was close to her mother, Oscar was definitely the favorite.

Unable to stop herself, Beatrice stood and threw the nearest thing, a cup, across the room. "This is ridiculous. Why would the man decide to marry me of all people? There were so many willing lasses throwing themselves at him."

The kiss. It had to be. Why had she been so foolish as to walk out in the garden with him? Obviously, after the effects of it, he'd not been thinking clearly. She looked to Oscar, who remained quiet, his eyes on the fire in the hearth. "Is there a possibility he'll change his mind by tomorrow?"

"No."

Her brother was not helping by brooding. She stalked over to him and punched his shoulder. "Are you going to Hardigg Castle? You don't have to."

His light brown eyes lifted to her and in them, she saw vulnerability. Something she'd rarely seen in her strong, brave brother. "I was to be lead guard here. At Hardigg Castle, I will have to prove myself again."

"There is no question about it then," Beatrice said. "You will remain here. However, you must help me find a way out of marrying that…that rogue."

In a very uncharacteristic way, Oscar stood and enveloped her in his arms. He kissed the top of her head and chuckled. "Dear sister, the man is so taken by you that I will have to say there isn't a way to convince him to change his mind. If I had to pick a husband for you, it would be someone who will come to love you and will treat you well. I do believe Gavin Mereworth is that man."

To keep him from seeing her tears, she pushed her

face into the rough fabric of his tunic. He was right, of course. Not about Gavin being the man for her, but that, in a case like this, it was not a horrible scenario. Admittedly, she was past the age to marry and had put her father off long enough.

"I will stop being a ninny then and prepare my things." After wiping her nose on his tunic, Beatrice stepped away and smiled up at her brother. He looked down on his clothing with a horrified expression. "Oh, don't act so annoyed. I'm sure you've had much worse spewed upon you."

When he chuckled and nodded, she went to her chambers to prepare.

"Everything is packed for you lass." Her maid opened a large truck that was filled with her clothes. "There is another smaller one there." The older woman pointed to the wall.

"I don't suppose you're coming with me?"

The older woman shook her head. "My husband and I will remain here. However, your mother has requested I send Grisilda with you," she replied, referring to her daughter who annoyed Beatrice. Grisilda had a screechy voice and was much too prying.

"Oh." She could not think of anything good to say about it, so Beatrice let out a breath. "Thank you for everything."

"I bid you farewell lass. May you be blessed with many young."

The woman shuffled away, sniffing and wiping her eyes, as Beatrice stood dumbfounded. Why anyone think a bunch of smelly children would be considered a blessing? She huffed and sat at her dressing table to unbraid her long hair.

THE NEXT DAY came with bright sunshine, gay bird song and a cheerful smile from her mother as she peered down at Beatrice. "Time to rise, my beautiful child. It's your wedding day."

That her parents had very little time to plan her nuptials didn't seem to bother them at all. They were probably too excited to be rid of their hellion daughter to grumble about it. Good thing the timing was short otherwise a parade from the village would have been organized.

Beatrice attempted to bat her mother away. "Your cheerfulness hurts my eyes. I am not in the mood to rise early today."

"Nonsense." The blankets were pulled away and her mother proceeded to pull her by the arms to sit. "Several village women will be arriving shortly. It is fortunate that Rose has a new gown she just made for Ina. Something good comes out of the misfortune of her intended leaving with the woman from the traveling peddler caravan. Of course, the poor girl wants nothing to do with the dress…"

As her mother continued rattling off the story of the gown, Beatrice managed to drink a cup of tea and trudge across the room to sit at her dressing table.

Within moments, as if by magic, she was surrounded by her mother's friends. They tugged at her hair, pinched her cheeks, dabbed her with powders and stuck flowers in her hair.

Two women who acted as if they carried God's very own sandals brought the gown in. Their faces reverent, they presented the gown to a roomful of accolades.

Rose beamed as she turned to Beatrice. "It's meant to be. The beautiful shades of autumn leaves are the perfect complement to your eyes, hair and complexion."

Since when had Rose become poetic? Beatrice pushed a flower at her temple out of the way to study the gown.

It was hideous.

To be fair, she'd never liked the color red. Her hair, complexion and eyes would not be brought out by the shade of crimson. Well, perhaps her eyes would, if she were honest. Perhaps a tear or two had been shed the night before after she'd gone to bed and her eyes felt very irritated at the moment. At least the neckline would keep her from accidentally spilling, unlike the dress from the night before.

At Rose expectant expression, Beatrice imitated the other women's initial reaction by gasping. "It's stunning. Thank you."

Beatrice was guided to stand and step into the gown, which was pulled up. Finally, the fastenings were tightened until she wondered how long it would be before passing out would be the only option.

"You look beautiful, dear." Her mother's face appeared behind her as Beatrice studied her reflection. The woman in the glass did not resemble her in the least. She had been painted, tugged and tucked. They'd changed her to look more like a gypsy than a bride. However, she had to admit the look was rather entertaining.

Hopefully, Gavin would be appalled and change his mind. She bit her bottom lip. No, it would embarrass her family. It was time to be mature and accept her fate. She was to become the Lady of Selkirk, married to Lord Gavin Mereworth, Duke of Selkirk.

"I hope he is a strong man who will be able to keep you in line," her mother mumbled with brows drawn. "I pray for him."

There were whispers of agreement and Beatrice gave her mother a flat look. Eyes hooded, she let out a breath. "Women should not be tamed by men, but rather accepted and given freedoms to be themselves."

Rose patted her arm. "Some women need to be tamed, dear. You cannot hope to continue in your wild ways. You will be a lady. Someone who, at all times must maintain decorum so as not to embarrass her husband."

Why did the woman have to go and make the day worse? If ever there was a reason for Gavin not to marry her that was it. As soon as they arrived at the keep, she would inform him of the huge mistake he was about to make.

# CHAPTER SIX

"**S**WEAR YOU NOW, on this sacred blade, that there is no reason known to you that this union should not proceed," The clergy said.

"I do swear"…" Gavin spoke the words without hesitation and was glad his voice held steady and strong. He was a duke, after all, and no matter what the circumstances of the rushed wedding, it was necessary his men present not question his stance.

Only Sinclair had dared question him on why the sudden marriage. He'd simply stated he wanted the wench and as she was from a family in good standing, it made perfect sense to marry her and not have the continued pestering to marry. Although his brother continued to suspect his uncles had something to do with it, he'd agreed that the feisty lass would, indeed, keep Gavin's attention.

His bride stood pale before him and he hated it. Although Beatrice kept her chin high, it trembled just enough for him to notice upon speaking her vows. Her eyes constantly searched his face as if he held the answer to why she suddenly found herself being married off to a total stranger.

Women, of course, had no say in whom they married. Not those of station anyway. Beatrice should have been prepared for eventually marrying someone of her father's choosing. That, however, did not make Gavin feel better. Most marriages did not happen for at least a fortnight, banns posted and all such nonsense. The time of betrothal would at least allow the bride to become accustomed to the idea of whom she'd be tied to for the rest of her life.

In this case, however, she'd only one night.

Their hands were brought together and the clergyman wrapped a red satin ribbon around them. The color matched her dress. He'd been alarmed at first seeing her, thinking she was someone else and that a cruel trick had been played upon him. It wasn't until she'd come closer that he'd realized someone had stained her cheeks and lips. The pout, already alluring, was even more so now that it was the color of ripe berries.

Truth be told, the part of the ceremony he looked

forward to the most was taking her body. Gavin had no doubt she'd enjoy bedsport, for she'd been quite eager the night before in the garden.

Although he'd insisted earlier there would be no witnesses at the bedding, his uncle, John, had disagreed and insisted there be at least two witnesses. The more proof the better he'd said to keep the Duke of Aldorf from arguing the marriage not to be valid.

What was next? An artist's depiction of the act?

His uncle John now stood beside him, pride gleaming as the exchange was finally completed. "Your father would be proud of your choice of a bride," the Lord stated, his gaze falling on Beatrice. "I do warn you, she is rather…unruly at times. However, she is quite a beauty."

The celebration meal was smaller than the night before, yet many townspeople remained an additional day to benefit from the second meal.

IT WAS LIKE a repeat of the night before, with almost everyone sitting in the same seats. The big difference was that now she sat next to Gavin at the high board. Beatrice sent a pointed look to the table where the glaring women continued to well…glare at her. She pictured shooting them between the eyes with her arrows and that helped ease her annoyance. Only a bit.

Gavin kept leaning to her and whispering in her ear. Each comment about how beautiful she looked and how eager he was to be alone with her made her stomach do strange things.

Too rattled to eat, she drank the sweetened mead and asked for a refill. One of the women suggested that if she drank enough, she would enjoy the bedding more.

Beatrice leaned back to peer down at Gavin's crotch. Elizabeth had said when a man was ready to mount a woman it would grow full and noticeable. The larger the bulge, the more it would hurt.

From what she gathered, it didn't seem too alarming. Then again, the dimness from the table made it hard to see.

She pulled her fork to the edge of the table, allowed it to fall and immediately bent at the waist to pick it up.

"I can get it." Gavin turned in his chair.

"No need, it's right here." She bent down and took a closer look. Her eyes rounded. There was a pronounced bulge between his legs.

When she straightened, she banged her head

against the table and several people turned to look just as a flower fell from her hair and plopped onto her plate. "I dropped my fork," she explained to no one in particular.

Gavin leaned into her ear. "In a few moments, you will be mine. Afterwards, you won't be so nervous around me."

A croak escaped and she picked up her glass, signaling the nearest maid for more drink.

"Come, dear." Her mother appeared out of nowhere and pulled Beatrice's shoulders. "It's time."

"But the music has barely begun and I need mead," Beatrice protested. "I hoped to dance."

"There is no time."

It didn't make any sense, from what she'd learned. The man speared the woman and once that was done, it was over. Horses and goats took, perhaps, a few seconds. So she imagined Gavin would take as long. Once that was done, it would be much too early to sleep.

"Mother," Beatrice hissed as she was led away from Gavin, who'd squeezed her hand. "Why the hurry?"

"It's your wedding night, dearest." The explanation was unnecessary. If anyone knew it was the night of her wedding, it was definitely she. "Your husband is eager to join with you."

Fortunately, the bedding preparation was not as elaborate as earlier. This time, her dress was removed, her hair brushed out and everyone had some sort of advice. From reciting poetry to keeping her eyes on the ceiling, each woman seemed to have a different take on what would happen once Gavin claimed her. Beatrice tugged a young maid's hand. The maid kept rolling her eyes at the running commentary. "Have you been with a man?"

The maid gave her a jaunty grin. "Aye, Milady."

"What is it like?"

"Honestly, Beatrice. She wouldn't know." Her mother attempted to intercede but Beatrice hushed her with a glare. "Would you all please leave?"

Finally, the women left, each giving her and the maid worried glances.

"What is your name?" Beatrice was anxious to hear what the girl would say, but decided to be a bit less obvious.

"Nora, Milady."

"Tell me." She sat up on the bed where the women had laid her with hair spread across the pillow. Now the effect was ruined, she imagined. No matter. As soon as Nora let them in, they'd return and push her back into the rather awkward and embarrassing position.

"My Neil is most wonderful, Milady. He takes me in such ways that send me to cry out with passion. First, he places his hand between my legs and moves his fingers round and round while he kisses me and prepares me for his hardened…"

"Enough." Beatrice's mother rushed in and moved to Nora. "That will be all. See that the men are made aware Beatrice is ready."

Once again, Beatrice was pushed back and the other women appeared. The discussion centered on who would witness the joining. It had been decided other than the Lord and the clergyman, her mother and Lady Mereworth would be in attendance.

There was a commotion at the door and the witnesses proceeded in. Her mother's friends dashed out and the room became quiet.

Beatrice refused to look at the gathered group. Instead, she lay still and kept her gaze on the ceiling, noting there was a very industrious spider in residence by the size of the webs that clung.

"Look at me." Gavin stood before her, fully dressed. His lips curved in reassurance. "I will make this as quick as possible."

He took her by the sides and pulled her to the bottom of the bed, which she figured ruined the effects of her hair on the pillow. But she was more worried about her sleeping gown sliding up past her hips than to think about other things.

When she attempted to push it down, he moved her hands away and spread her knees. Then, pushing his britches down, he took his staff in hand and settled between her legs.

Gavin's face was like a stone. He glanced to the gathered group. "I will take Beatrice's body to be my own. When I pierce her maidenhead, our union will be consummated and I expect it will be enough to pronounce our marriage valid."

Gavin looked from witness to witness. "I am a vigorous man. I will ensure to continue my bloodline and bring children to this marriage."

Beatrice's rounded eyes went to his sex. It looked much too large not to hurt. She attempted to push her legs together, but his hips were in the way. "No."

His eyes locked to hers and she struggled to push

away. "Be still wife." He pushed into her body without warning and Beatrice screamed at the piercing pain. Unable to move as he held her in place, she dug her nails into the bedding as tears slid down the sides of her face.

The pain began to recede and she wanted to beg him not to pull out, not to move. The damned man pulled out and spread her blood onto the blanket.

"The maidenhead has been torn. Beatrice is mine."

In that moment, she hated not only Gavin, but also her parents and all men.

"Be still." He pushed back inside her and although it was uncomfortable, it didn't hurt as much.

"Leave us." Her husband issued the command over his shoulder and remained over her until they left.

"Will you please get out of me now?" Beatrice snapped. "It's uncomfortable."

"No. I have to show you what lovemaking is. I will not let this night pass with you looking at me like that."

He struggled a bit and somehow removed his tunic so that he was naked as the day he was born.

"Relax, little bird. Allow me to love you and show you what I can do with such a delightful body as yours."

It was rather awkward to have a conversation with a naked man who remained between her legs. Beatrice, however, found it was hard to look away from his well-formed chest. She allowed her gaze to travel across it and up to his face.

Her husband's lips curled right before covering hers with a kiss so impassioned, she lost her ability to think. How could so many sensations come about from just a kiss?

When Gavin began moving, his shaft sliding out and then in, Beatrice tensed.

"Relax, let me love you," he urged. His breathy voice at her ear did, indeed, have a relaxing affect. His mouth, once again, moved over hers before trailing kisses and nips down to her throat. The ministrations sent tingles down her spine.

Beatrice raked her nails down his back when he pushed her gown away to gain access to her breasts and suckled first at one then the other.

All the while, Gavin's length slid in and out. With each movement, she wanted more. She wanted him to move faster. Beatrice grabbed his buttocks with both hands, urging him.

He lifted up and peered down at her, his face

flushed and the tendons at his neck taut. "I will ensure you peak before I do. I want to watch as you dissolve under me."

With his gaze locked on hers, Gavin thrust and pulled back over and over again. His lips parted as he held back for her.

Beatrice lost control and began to flail at whatever happened. A streak of heat, which had pooled where they were joined traveled up her torso and down her legs until her toes curled and she cried out.

While dazed in pleasure, his hoarse moan filled the room and then Gavin collapsed over Beatrice, his body trembling.

# CHAPTER SEVEN

W HEN MORNING ARRIVED, Beatrice pretended to remain asleep. She didn't want to face Gavin and allow him the opportunity to gloat over how he'd completely owned her in so many ways. Just thinking about what they'd done in the darkness of the chamber brought heat to her face and immediately her breath hitched.

The pulse between her legs would be a constant reminder that day of being someone's wife now. Beatrice hoped it would ease. Although the night before had been quite enjoyable, the discomfort of her first time lingered now.

There was a discreet knock at the door and Gavin stirred. "Enter." His groggy voice made Beatrice grin like a loon. She let out a breath and turned away from the door, not ready to face whoever entered.

"Your Grace." A man, probably his squire, had entered. "The bath will be set up for the lady. And a tray of tea and light repast as you requested."

For the next few moments, there was shuffling and the sound of water and dishes being set out. Gavin pulled Beatrice back against his side and nuzzled her neck.

"Wake up, beauty. You will feel better if you bathe in warm water."

The idea of bathing in front of him made her uncomfortable. "Can you leave while I do so?"

His chuckle was soft and sensual. "I would not take you for being shy. I have seen you. All of you."

If he didn't stop talking, she'd ignore the pain and demand he take her again. Beatrice turned to face him. Unfortunately, her hair wrapped around her head, so it took a bit of tugging by them both before she could see him.

"I am not used to anyone in the room while I bathe. My maid usually leaves me alone so I can wash and such."

"Hmmm." His reply was noncommittal.

When he slid from the bed, Beatrice thought he'd dress and leave. Instead, he scooped her up and carried her to the tub and climbed in.

"What are you doing?" Beatrice demanded, her

eyes round. "We can't do this."

With a bit of trouble, he lowered and settled her between his legs, back against his chest.

Admittedly, the heated water helped her discomfort. However, a man bathing with her was not something she'd heard of when it came to marriage. Would they have to do everything together?

"Are we going to always bathe together?"

Once again, he chuckled. "Would you like us to?"

"I don't think so." When he tensed, she amended her declaration. "Every once in a while would be nice. But not after hunting or such when we will be so soiled."

"You won't have to worry about that," Gavin said as he reached for a bar of soap and began sliding it over her skin. "You are a lady now and, as such, your outdoor activities will be limited to targets. Archery is fine. Hunting, however, is not."

Water splashed over the sides as Beatrice scrambled to get out. Not caring that she was fully nude and dripping wet, she stood beside the tub with hands fisted and her jaw clenched.

"I will not be sitting about indoors for the rest of my days, Gavin Mereworth. Nor will I stop hunting.

You cannot keep me locked away like some…some…"

"Lady?" He pressed his lips together forming a thin line and gave her a pointed look. "Like it or not, you married a duke. There are certain expectations that come with…"

"I don't care about expectations." She stomped to where her dressing gown had been discarded.

The sound of water followed by a groan made her look to see Gavin now stood next to the tub. "As my wife, you will obey me. Did you not pay any attention to the vows?"

"I was too busy trying to figure out why I was there," Beatrice snapped. She looked around the room trying to decide whether to get dressed and leave the chamber or toss him out. "Please leave. I need time to get dressed, unless we have to do that together, as well."

"I'm naked." Gavin's half-closed eyes and flat lips, as if bored, made her want to slap him. "Once we finish bathing, I will get dressed and we will discuss expectations over tea." He motioned to the teapot as if she were too daft to understand.

She had not rinsed and half of her hair was wet. "I do need to finish bathing. My hair is…oh, never mind.

Why am I explaining myself to you?"

Without waiting for him, she went back to the bath and sunk into the water. Once her hair was wet, she washed with haste, ignoring Gavin who attempted to squeeze himself into the tight space.

"I can understand how you must feel. There is a reason for my having to marry with so much haste. I will explain it to you when the time is right." He lifted a pitcher. "Let me help you rinse your hair."

Once she was clean, Beatrice climbed back out and dried off before donning her dressing gown. She poured the tea. From the corner of her eye, Gavin's actions kept her attention.

He scrubbed his body, and then washed his shoulder-length hair. Afterwards, he stood and bent to dip the pitcher into the clean bucket of water next to the tub. His form was, without question, the most beautiful she had ever seen. With his eyes closed as he poured water over his head, Beatrice could study him at leisure.

At remembering what his body and hers had done the night before, a flush rose to her cheeks.

It was a pity she was about to argue with the handsome man until he'd probably want to toss her out the window.

GRISILDA PRACTICALLY FLOATED around Beatrice, pinning her braid around her head. "I am so excited at moving with you to a castle. It's so much larger than this estate, I am told.

"It could mean it's hideous," Beatrice snapped. Her cowardly husband had yanked on his tunic and britches and rounded her to escape before she could broach the subject of hunting again.

Now she'd have to wait until a moment alone to ensure he understood there were no plans on her part to stop hunting. Her entire life, she'd been part of the local hunts and had participated in every competition. She was one of the best archers in the land.

"Beatrice...I apologize, Milady," Grisilda flushed. "I cannot become used to calling you by the title. Although I will learn. I promise."

Waving away any concern, Beatrice was anxious to leave the chamber. "No matter, I don't believe in titles, not in this case anyway. What is it?"

"I am wondering if perhaps your brother is traveling as well."

Almost daily, women who pined over Oscar approached her. Now that she considered it, no one had been clear about whether he'd remain or not. Her mother had been cheerful that morning, which led her to the conclusion he'd decided to remain. However, with the marriage, bedding and having a new husband, she'd forgotten to ask.

"I am not sure. Have you seen him about?"

Grisilda's long sigh made Beatrice smack her arm. "For goodness' sake, will you reply to my question?"

"Yes, he is here. He broke his fast in the great room with the guardsmen."

Tired of whatever primping Grisilda continued to perform, Beatrice stood. "I will go down and speak to him." She hesitated. "What of my husband?"

"He left with the Lord and his brother. They mounted and headed away from the village. I do believe they plan to visit several farmers today."

So Gavin had left her to fend for herself. Today, she'd not only face the Lord's wife alone, but also the other women and guardsmen. "Perhaps I should remain here. I am a bit tired."

Grisilda's eyes narrowed and her brows joined. "Lady Alice asked to be notified when you left your chambers. She plans to meet you at the high board."

"Did you just make that up?" Beatrice tugged Grisilda's hair.

The young woman yelped and swatted away her hand. "We cannot continue to act like at your home. You can't hit me or tug my hair anymore." Grisilda yanked Beatrice's ear. "Nor can I do that anymore."

It wasn't becoming for the duke's new wife to be fighting with her maid. However, Beatrice couldn't help but grin as she rushed to the door. "Grisilda, don't be a ninny. Ladies hit their maids all the time. Now hurry, go inform the lord's wife I am heading to the great room now."

"If you hit me I will hit you back," Grisilda spouted as she hurried away.

EVERY HEAD TURNED when she entered the room. Damn Gavin for not being there to face them alongside her. Then again, he'd faced whoever was there earlier. At least the Lord and his strange brother were gone. Somehow, it felt different as she nodded in acknowledgement at the same guards she'd ignored just two days earlier.

Her brother was not at the table. "Where is Oscar?" she asked Finlay, the only male who dared look directly at her.

Finlay stood and bowed at the waist. "He's gone to relieve himself, Milady. I can go fetch him if you wish."

Snatching his arm, she tugged him away from the table. "What are you doing? Why did you bow?"

"I am not sure," Finlay said, ignoring the snickers from the guards. "You are a lady now. A duke's wife. Do you know they are second in line to the throne?"

By the time one went through all the dukes, it would take a plague of enormous magnitude for Gavin to become king. However, Beatrice understood what Finlay meant. Her husband's title was, indeed, a very grand one.

She smiled at her friend. "I will miss you, Finlay. Never change." Over his shoulder, she spotted her brother. Unfortunately, Alice Mereworth entered at the same time.

The lord's wife was, without a doubt, one of the dullest people Beatrice had ever met. Although only about thirty and five or so, the woman moved like she was ancient. Her shoulders curved and although her clothes were well made, they were of a brown color that somehow blended with the walls and rushes upon the floor.

It was difficult not to yawn just by studying the woman. Beatrice hurried to join Lady Alice, who settled into a chair. "How are you, Beatrice? I trust you rested well."

"Well, yes. However it's strange to sleep with a man in the bed."

The woman gave her a blank look that made Beatrice wonder if perhaps Lady Alice was still asleep. "I agree. I rarely slept those first nights."

"Yes, well, I have to admit to not sleeping much last night." Beatrice hid a smile by tearing a piece of bread and eating it. "Do you know when we are to leave?"

"Oh no. I am not kept informed of such things." The woman placed a cool hand on Beatrice's lower arm. "You shouldn't worry yourself. Let your husband inform you of what he considers you should know."

Hopefully, the woman took her silence as acquiescence. In truth, she was picturing running to the garden where she could scream. How did a man like Lord Mereworth, who was so vibrant, stand spending day after day in this woman's company?

A maid neared with trenchers laden with meats and cheese. One was placed before Beatrice and a second, half the size, before Lady Alice.

"My appetite is quite small these days," the woman explained. "I tire of eating at times."

"My mother says that once I am older I will grow round from eating so much. I love eating." Beatrice demonstrated by tearing a large bite from the meat, following it with cheese and then washing it all down with her tea. She looked to the maid. "Can you bring me some of the sweets from last night?"

Beatrice paused, lost in thought for a moment. "I need to eat if my husband expects what happened last night to happen again." Before she could continue speaking, the lord's wife gasped and covered her mouth with one hand. "You enjoyed it?"

Although she'd been told repeatedly not to speak her mind, Beatrice found it was hard not to. Frankness, in her opinion, should be a virtue.

"I did enjoy bedsport with Gavin. Very much more than I expected, actually. I do believe my husband has done it many times before. Otherwise, how would he have known what to do? If I'd known how enjoyable it was, perhaps I'd have married long ago or at least sought out a handsome lad or two." Beatrice laughed at her own joke. "I wonder how many lovers Gavin has had up to now."

Wide eyed, Lady Mereworth clutched the crucifix handing from her neck. She leaned away as if afraid of contracting a disease.

"Beatrice!" Oscar had somehow materialized next to the table. "I hear you need to speak to me immediately?" His pointed look was followed by him holding out a hand toward her. "Come with me, Milady."

"I'm hungry," Beatrice offered weakly. Her brother's lectures tended to be long. Her food would be cold or gone before she returned.

Giving up, as Oscar didn't budge, Beatrice looked toward the lord's wife who swallowed visibly. "We must have tea later."

Beatrice grabbed a chunk of bread and cheese before allowing Oscar to lead her away.

"Are you mad?" Her brother whirled to face her as soon as they arrived in the gardens. "Did mother not speak to you about Lady Alice?"

What had happened to everyone this morning? They all acted as if she'd not lived there for years already. "I know she's dull and boring. She's been the same for years. I am trying to be her friend. Since I have to live here now, it would be good to get to know her better."

Oscar let out a long breath. "I suppose you rarely came to the keep before now." He looked toward the doorway. "Lady Alice asked to be sent to a convent to live out the rest of her days. She claims to have heard from God that she is not to be married. It is rare she leaves the confines of her chambers, but did so today because of you. I suppose the Lord demanded it."

"That makes no sense. Why would anyone voluntarily go to a convent? Have you seen the excuses they use for beds? The food is nothing but porridge and they all have such a dour disposi..." Beatrice glanced over her shoulder. "Then again, I can picture it."

Oscar shook his head. "I do not understand why the duke chose you. If anything, you become more unruly by the day."

"I must ask." Beatrice pulled him further away from the building. "Why did he choose me? Why such a hurry to marry?"

Her brother would never divulge anything he overheard. Over the years, she'd given up asking anything. On rare occasions, Oscar would speak to their father about things, but it was only when whatever was said would become known by all.

"If I'd known earlier, I would have talked the man

out of it." Her brother let out a frustrated breath. "I wonder the same. Not so much why he married you as I don't want to imagine what you did to gather his attention, but why the hurry."

"I did not do anything."

"Please try to be more…I don't know, docile."

It was best to ignore the request as she planned to argue with Gavin when she saw him next. "What did you decide? Will you come with me?"

Oscar's face softened and he cupped her jaw. "It's best that I do, little beastie."

She kicked his shin and dashed away, screaming with glee when he chased after her.

GAVIN STOOD AT the balcony. With a piece of bread in her hand and her hair falling from its braids, his wife raced around the garden being chased by her brother. The huge man caught up to her and swung her around. Beatrice's laughter made Gavin smile. How he hoped he'd not ruin her spirit.

It was imperative she became with child soon, which meant he'd bed her often.

That, in and of itself, would be quite enjoyable. However, what would happen if she found out the only reason he married her was because he needed an heir or two to keep the threat of losing his title at bay?

How would the sprite react?

"You must take Beatrice under control. Her behavior is most unbecoming of a lady." Coming to stand beside him, Alice sniffed and looked out to where the siblings now walked side by side, talking. "She spoke rather brashly of your night, loudly exclaiming her enjoyment. I am shocked that you would marry someone like her."

Just then, Beatrice looked to where he stood. Her wide gaze moved from him to Alice. Beatrice stopped walking and the now crumbling bread fell from her hand.

"I would say it's exactly why I married her. To marry someone dull, who prefers to sit alone than to share my life, would be worse than hell itself." He walked away, ignoring the dour woman's gasp.

# CHAPTER EIGHT

S INCLAIR CAUGHT UP with Gavin near the stables where he instructed his guards to prepare for their return to Hardigg Castle.

"I am ready to return. It's been long enough of a dalliance here." His brother walked to his horse and held out a carrot.

"Have you already plundered through all the women in the village, Brother?" Gavin shook his head when his brother grinned. "I am quite ready to return, as well."

"Have you told your wife? Are you prepared for the forthcoming first time leaving dramatic farewell scene with her family?"

If he were to be honest, he'd been avoiding Beatrice. From the fire in her gaze, it was obvious she planned a row and he wasn't sure how he would deflect her wishes without a huge argument. He'd have to be stern with her about certain things, but give her enough freedoms so not to break her spirit.

After several more instructions to the guards, Gavin asked Sinclair to walk with him.

"I am perplexed when it comes to Beatrice," he admitted. "She wants to continue to hunt and traipse about the forest. I am not sure what to do about it."

Of course, his brother was the least suitable to give marriage advice. But he trusted Sinclair and knew his brother had the best intentions when it came to the family.

Sinclair smiled. "The reason you married her was exactly this. Lady Beatrice will always be a challenge. One of your best decisions, Brother. However, in this case, you must be strong. She cannot run free and such. Someone could see it as an opportunity to harm her."

The thought of harm coming to his new wife bothered him. True, he'd not known her long, but he was rapidly growing to care for Beatrice.

"Not to mention if rumor is spread of her freedoms, Aldorf could use it as an opportunity to cast doubt if and when she is with child," Sinclair added.

HE FOUND BEATRICE back in their bedroom. She sat in a chair next to the fireplace sharpening a dagger with a stone. Not exactly a scene a man expects to walk into the day after his wedding.

"Lady Alice informed me I must speak to you regarding your lack of decorum." He walked closer and peered down at his wife, who ignored him. "Beatrice, what did you say to her?"

His wife let out a huff. "She asked if I slept well last night. I told her no. In making conversation, I described why."

"I see. You did expect she'd be shocked by your frank speech did you not?"

Beatrice didn't reply right away. Instead, she put the dagger down and looked into the fire. "I'm not sorry I did it. She described bedsport as unpleasant and I corrected her." Her lips curved and he knew she thought about Alice's shocked expression.

It was hard not to smile in relief that she'd enjoyed their first night enough to brag about it. "So you don't consider it unpleasant then? I am glad to hear it. However, in the future, keep any conversation about what happens in our bed between us."

"No."

"What?"

"I will probably share with a good friend. Once I

find one in Hardigg."

It was hard not to laugh. "Very well."

"About hunting…" she began, her nostrils flaring and her chin lifted in challenge. "We did not finish our conversation earlier."

"We leave tomorrow, Beatrice. I came to fetch you so we can travel to the village and say farewell to your parents."

Beatrice's lips parted and she blinked several times. "So soon?"

He was rather proud of his deflection.

"I will call Grisilda to ensure my things are packed right away." Beatrice got to her feet and studied him. "Why is everything so rushed? I feel as if there is a secret I am not privy to."

Gavin took her by the arms and pulled her closer. "I wanted a wife. Although I didn't plan to marry so soon, once meeting you, there was no doubt in my mind. As far as returning to Hardigg, it was planned for us to leave soon since I have matters to attend to there."

With her head turned away, she slid a look up to him and pursed her lips. "How clever you are to have a reply for everything so quickly. I wonder if, perhaps, you plan every conversation before entering into it. I was told by Oscar, earlier, that you'd told him it was possible the visit would be extended. Why the change?"

Damn. He'd forgotten the conversation with the brother when he'd asked to join Gavin's guard. "Tis true. However, after discussing things with my brother earlier, he reminded me it was not prudent to remain gone from Hardigg overlong."

"Is there a threat of some kind?"

The woman was not only beautiful, but also intelligent.

"Wife, there are always threats when one is lord. Unfortunately, my title makes it even worse." He pulled his wife against him and covered her mouth with his. Not just to quiet her questions, but because his desire for her rose more and more with each exchange.

When she softened against his chest and parted her lips to allow him entrance, Gavin feared losing control. He couldn't take her again this soon; she'd be sore after her first time. However, he would barely be able to wait for the night after.

Three swift knocks forced him to tear his lips away from Beatrice. She didn't move away and he wrapped his arms around her. "Enter."

Sinclair pushed past the door and smiled at him knowingly. "Our uncle requests that we come to his study."

Without moving away from a now squirming Beatrice, Gavin pressed a kiss to her temple. "Is something amiss?"

"I believe it has to do with our imminent departure." Sinclair looked to Beatrice. "I apologize, Lady Beatrice." Sinclair lowered his head in greeting. "I hope my brother treats you well."

Gavin glared at Sinclair's most inopportune comment and let out a low groan when Beatrice pushed away.

"He treats me well. However, we will be discussing any plans to keep me from hunting and such. I suggest you speak to him about it. If I remember correctly, I bested you in competition once."

Sinclair pressed his lips together, but it was obvious he was attempting not to grin. "I will endeavor to convince Gavin to see the error of his ways."

Not convinced, Beatrice huffed and went to the wardrobe. She began pulling gowns out and putting them on the bed. "Please send Grisilda to me. You can probably find her atop a stairwell or window some-where lurking around Oscar like a bird of prey."

At her comment, Sinclair let out a loud guffaw and Gavin coughed to cover his chuckle. "I will, wife."

# CHAPTER NINE

*Central Cumbria, England*

THE HORSES CANTERED along at a steady pace. Beatrice rode directly behind the impressive front Gavin and Oscar made. On either side of her and behind were her new husband's guards. Just ahead of the party rode two guardsmen ensuring their safety. Sinclair rode alongside the wagon carrying trunks and Grisilda, maintaining a close distance.

Gavin turned to look at her and pointed to the distance. "It's not a long ride to my home, just over half a day's ride."

There was an eager shine to his gaze and his lips curved. "Let me know if you need to rest or stop at anytime. I will help you dismount."

Beatrice nodded, knowing he asked to be sure she'd not spring from the horse like a wildling.

AFTER SEVERAL HOURS, they stopped to rest. The respite

didn't last long and once again they mounted to continue on their way. It would be another three hours, at least, to the Hardigg Castle. Although the lands had a resemblance to her home, this area near the sea was plush with high cliffs. She inhaled the sea air and wondered what her new home would be like.

They traveled along a trail for several hours before stopping to give the horses a break. Glad for it, Beatrice allowed a guard to help her dismount and hurried to the back of the wagon. Once she gathered her bow and quiver, she and Grisilda went into the forest to relieve themselves.

"WHAT IS THAT?" Beatrice stopped as they were walking back to the horses. "Did you hear it?" She yanked Grisilda to the ground. "Someone is about."

"Stop there! Do not advance!" one of the guards called out to whoever neared their party.

From where they hid, Beatrice could see three men approach Gavin and Oscar.

Everyone wore stoic expressions. Whoever the visitors were, they were not friends.

"We come in peace, Your Grace," a bearded man with dirty, long hair stated, holding up a hand in greeting. "I am guard to the Duke of Aldorf. I was, in fact, heading toward Lord Mereworth's lands to bring his message after learning you were not here."

Beatrice looked behind her and then to the sides. The three men were not alone. There was a strange hush in the surroundings. Birds were unusually silent. Surely their guardsmen and Gavin had noticed.

"I am heading to my home. You can bring the message there. Right now, I am not stopping for talk."

"He knows," Beatrice whispered to Grisilda who paled.

"Knows what?" Grisilda replied, her voice barely audible.

The stranger bowed his head in thought and then looked up. "Unfortunately, I have my orders and cannot wait for your invite…" he left the word hanging.

"Who are you and what do you want?" Gavin snapped.

"Archibald Brown, guard to the Duke of Aldorf." When Sinclair pulled his sword, the stranger snarled. "I hoped not to have to kill you on this day, Your Grace."

Beatrice immediately yanked an arrow from her quiver and waited. Grisilda flattened on the ground with muffled breaths of alarm.

A loud battle cry sounded. Beatrice wasn't sure who it was.

Then she heard Oscar's angry growl followed by metal against metal as he clashed with one of the men behind Brown. The other horseman landed on the ground with a thud with Sinclair over him. Still atop his horse, her brother had grabbed the other guard and held his sword across the man's neck. "Tell them to cease at once."

The speaker seemed to gain boldness. "And if I don't?"

GAVIN PRAYED HIS wife would stay in place wherever she was hidden. Aldorf's messenger, who he figured was actually a mercenary and not a guard under Aldorf's employ, had others with him who remained hidden.

The man slid a warning look to Oscar and Sinclair before meeting Gavin's gaze. "We plan no harm upon you. The duke sends a clear message. You will not fight the loss of your title."

The man was either well accompanied or daft. Gavin's guardsmen surrounded Brown. He'd never survive any attempt against him.

"I am not in fear. However, I must warn you. My men have not seen battle recently. They are blood-thirsty."

When Archibald leaned forward as if to strike him, an arrow was impaled on a tree just above the man's head.

Everyone looked toward the forest where Beatrice stood with a second arrow already set. "I won't miss next time. Tell the rest of your men to leave unless you wish this arrow through your right eye."

The man looked to Gavin for confirmation.

"She never misses."

"We didn't threaten you in any manner." The stranger leaned away and held his hands up. He whistled and there was rustling followed by horsemen riding away. There were only two and Gavin wondered if any were left behind hoping not to be found out.

The second arrow flew so close to the stranger's head, it sliced the side of his temple.

"I was not aware that gentlemen allowed their women to wage their battles." Spittle flew from the man's mouth as he wiped at the blood.

Beatrice was magnificent, her bow already holding

a third arrow. "All of them," she called out.

Gavin exchanged looks with his guardsmen who awaited his order to attack and find whoever hid in the trees. He considered that if someone struck his wife with an arrow at the moment, perhaps, it would make the situation less humiliating. Did she really think they needed her assistance?

"Beatrice, put the bow down." Gavin motioned to his men, who rushed into the trees. Whoever remained hidden would not live long. Archibald looked between Gavin and Beatrice in hopes she would listen to his command.

Finally, she lowered the bow and the man let out a breath. "I meant no harm, Your Grace." Those were his last words as the man fell dead to the ground.

Gavin wiped the blood from his sword. He looked to the pair his brother and Oscar held down. "Go back to Aldorf. Tell him I am married and with a son on the way. And tell him I got his message before killing his useless messenger."

The men galloped away.

Sinclair's flat gaze tracked the men who fled. "I trust our scouts got the others."

"Yes. Here they come now," Gavin replied, having

caught sight of his guards. Without a word, he turned his horse and began the trek home. It was best not to speak to Beatrice at the moment. His guard would demand he punish her and as much as he hated to do so, it was necessary.

Oscar caught up to him. "I apologize for my sister's behavior, Your Grace. I can punish her if you wish."

"No. As her husband, it is my duty." He looked to the worried brother and softened. "Other than not being able to sit easily for a few days, I won't harm her badly."

"That is less than I planned," Oscar gritted out.

HARDIGG CASTLE WAS, indeed, grand. Beatrice studied the huge grey walls that surrounded it as they neared. Since they'd mounted and commenced their trek after the guards and Gavin dispatched with the men back in the forest, neither Oscar nor Gavin had spoken to her. The guards remained impassive, their flat gazes going to her every so often.

She'd made a huge mistake. In attempting to show her abilities and lack of fear, she'd embarrassed her husband and brother. Not only that, but any argument to be allowed to hunt would now fall on deaf ears.

Beatrice let out a sigh and wondered what her punishment would be. Left to Oscar, he'd lock her in a room with only bread and water for days. It never lasted longer than two days, really, as her mother would sneak her food. Her father was always more lenient and that, perhaps, was the problem. She'd grown up not knowing her place as a woman.

Once they crossed a bridge over a moat, the forward guard arrived at the gates and called out to the men atop. The huge gates opened to a village. Beatrice forgot about her woes as she took in all the activity. She'd never known a castle so large it held an entire community within its walls.

They rode two by two as curious villagers scurried over to greet their Lord and study her and Oscar. Of course, the women instantly transformed into giggling and whispering simpletons once noticing her brother's handsome face.

Beatrice also gathered interest. Several men called out to Gavin to ask about her. Her husband softened visibly once surrounded by his people. "A grand feast is planned, spread the word. Two days hence we will celebrate my marriage to Lady Beatrice."

The news was received with gasps of surprise and

loud murmurings. Lads and lasses dashed off to be the first ones to spread the news.

Several women waved at Beatrice and she returned their friendly acknowledgments with a smile and lift of her hand. Although she wasn't sure what to expect once they arrived at the keep, at least she could look forward to eating in two days.

A second set of gates, not as high as the others, was opened allowing them into a smaller courtyard. This area was like that of the Castle Lansing. However, she noted that every area was well maintained and much tidier.

Stable hands rushed forward to help with the horses. Despite wanting to climb down, she remained mounted waiting for Gavin.

After a few words to the guards and hands, her husband walked towards her. His long strides assured and his shoulders straight. He looked up to her and lifted his hands circling her waist. Without a word, he lowered her to the ground, allowing very little space between them so that she was forced to slide against him. The feel of his hard body took her breath away and Beatrice swallowed. Hopefully, he wouldn't send her away from his bed. She yearned for him, as they'd not made love since the first night.

"After we go inside and I introduce you to the household staff, we will go to our chamber and speak." He took her arm, leading her toward the front doors.

For the first time, Beatrice was scared. There had been no warmth in either his eyes or his touch. When speaking, his voice held an angry edge. From the corner of her eyes, she slid a peek at him. Gavin kept a neutral expression, eyes straight ahead.

Just inside the doorway, along the wall, a line of people greeted them. After being introduced to the head mistress and cook, Beatrice moved down the line ensuring to speak to each person individually. She repeated their names back and committed to memory their faces as much as possible.

"Come, we must speak," Gavin spoke into her ear as he guided her to a stairwell. They climbed up the stairs and, with each step, her heart pounded harder. She wanted to yank her arm away, race to a room and slam the door behind her. However, this was their first day before his people and every set of eyes in the great room followed them.

It took all her inner strength, but Beatrice kept a pleasant expression, forcing the corners of her mouth to curve upward. Head held high, she racked her brain for how to apologize and what to say to her husband in hopes it would lessen his anger.

Finally, they entered a grand chamber. A large bed with what looked to be newly made coverings was against the far wall across from a fireplace. In front of the fireplace were two chairs. Obviously, Gavin had sent word of his upcoming nuptials as soon as he'd asked for her hand in marriage.

"Remain standing." At his curt order, Gavin took her cloak from her shoulders and maneuvered her to stand beside a chair.

A tremor shook her, so Beatrice grasped her hands together.

With what seemed to be calculating moves, Gavin took a leather strap from beside the fireplace and walked to her. "This is not at all how I hoped our life together here would commence. I do not wish to punish you, Beatrice. I hate that it is not only expected of me, but that you have forced my hand in it."

"I-I am not sure what I was thinking. I reacted out of fear..."

"Don't lie to me," Gavin snapped. Beatrice stiffened and held her breath. "There wasn't one ounce of fear in you as you stood with your arrow aimed at the messenger. Not only that, you didn't have any regard for the fact you made a very open target for anyone behind you."

She'd not considered it. "Oh."

"Yes. That is all you can say. Please refrain from any explanations as I do not have the patience for them right now."

He moved to a chair and looked down at it and then at her. "Bend over the back of the chair."

"What are you doing? No. I won't do it." Panicked, she looked to the doorway only to gasp at seeing her brother with his arms crossed, blocking any chance of escape.

"Do as your husband asks, Beatrice. Do not humiliate our family further." The disappointment in her brother's expression tore her apart and she practically threw herself over the back of the chair.

It was obvious Gavin did not use as much force as he could have behind the swift strikes on her exposed bottom, yet each strike burned, sending pain down her legs. Despite the pain being tolerable, Beatrice couldn't stop from crying. Not only did she feel shamed by her actions but also, at the same time, she felt betrayed by the two men who she'd tried to protect. Her overzealousness had led to this. However, she wasn't sure how this would impact her feelings toward Gavin.

The last strike seemed harder and Beatrice cried out as her overly sensitive skin felt as if it split.

"I will send Grisilda to see about you. Remain here until tomorrow. A meal will be brought up," Gavin said in a stoic voice. He dropped the leather strap and stalked out of the room, slamming the door.

TORQUIL ROBERTS HAD been his father's closest advisor and friend. Although only nine and thirty, he was wise beyond his years. The formidable warrior came from a tragic life of being bastard born to a Lord who denied him for many years. As a young babe, he'd scraped by begging for food until the Lord finally took pity. He'd come to live at Hardigg years earlier and soon became a trusted friend of the family and had served as the head of Gavin's father's guard.

Upon Gavin's introduction to Oscar, both large males had sized one another up for a moment before shaking hands. They would become fast friends. Of that, Gavin had no doubt, as they were similar in personality.

"I hear you came upon trouble on your way here," Torquil said, settling with a glass of whisky. "I also hear your wife defended your honor." There was a slight twitch to his lips, which made Gavin squeeze his own cup tight.

There would be much talk of what happened since he didn't doubt the guards would discuss it. Afterwards, their families would hear about it.

"I punished her. However, I must speak again to her about it. I'm not sure how to handle the lass. She's a spirited one."

Oscar cleared his throat. "It is my and my father's fault. We allowed her too much freedom."

"Tis not a fault for a woman to be spirited. I don't believe Gavin would have married her otherwise," Sinclair stated from the doorway.

Torquil shook his head. "However, you must find a way to, I don't know, perhaps control her in ways that won't be harmful to her nature."

The warm whisky worked itself down his throat as Gavin wondered what Beatrice was doing at the moment. She had cried. He'd not expected it. It made him feel a louse for striking her. Had Oscar not been at the door, prepared to punish her himself, he'd have spared her after the first two strikes.

"I am all ears," he said to Torquil who refilled everyone's glass. "Of course, none of you have wives, so I doubt you can help me."

The men nodded in acknowledgment and Gavin decided he'd have supper here in the study and finish the rest of the whisky.

# CHAPTER TEN

*Hardigg Castle, Carlisle, Central Cumbia, England*

THE EVENING CAME soon since they'd arrived at the keep after midafternoon. Grisilda assisted Beatrice in unpacking. Afterwards, Beatrice took a hot bath. Although she suspected her maid knew what happened, the usually inquisitive woman spoke only about the travel and about settling in to her own room. "It's very nice and the other maids here have been so friendly to me. They ask questions about you as expected," Grisilda explained.

"I'm tired. Can you add a log to the fire?" Beatrice asked as she went to the bed. "Good night. I hope you rest well."

"And you." Grisilda hugged her and, after doing as requested, left the room.

Aside from the glow of the fire, one lantern remained lit for when Gavin returned. Beatrice lay in bed and gingerly touched her bottom and found it only smarted a bit.

The silence was broken when the door opened. Gavin sent his squire away, insisting he did not require assistance. There was some shuffling as he undressed and her husband slid into bed and promptly fell asleep.

It was a while later that she realized how hurt she truly was. As much as she didn't wish to resent him, it was hard not to be hurt that he'd struck her when she'd tried to help.

THE FOLLOWING MORNING, the room was starkly silent. Gavin's side of the bed was empty and the air chilled. By the dimness outside the window, it was either cloudy or still very early. Beatrice slid to the edge of the bed and, donned a robe. She them walked to the window to peer outside.

The guard was assembled. In front of them, Gavin and a man she'd not met before stood side by side. Oscar stood with the guardsmen on the front line.

She leaned forward to get a better look. The man that stood beside Gavin was tall in stature with wisps of grey at his temples.

Gavin paced as he spoke. He looked from one end of the lineup of men to the other. Once he finished speaking, the men disbanded and she moved back. He'd not said anything about her being banished, that she had to remain in the chambers, however, mortified over having caused any kind of embarrassment toward her brother and husband made it difficult to face anyone as yet.

"I came to see about you." Grisilda entered with her usual brisk pace. After a quick assessment of the wardrobe, the maid pulled a serviceable gown from it and placed it on the bed. "Once you finish washing your face, I will help you dress and see about your hair. Molly, the headmistress, is anxious for you to walk through the kitchen and such."

Of course, she had to see about the household and begin the process of asserting herself as the lord's wife. That was the reason her husband had not punished her by ordering her to remain in the chambers, even though he had to have known it would be a worse punishment than any strikes to her bottom.

She lived for fresh air. Being outdoors was like a second home to her.

THE KITCHEN WAS large and pristine. Beatrice walked about peering into pots and ensuring to praise Molly and her two helpers, who beamed with pride at her constant exclamations of approval.

"Milady, I pride myself on our garden." Molly motioned to a doorway. "Would you care to walk outside?"

"Of course," Beatrice exclaimed with delight. "I'm anxious to see it. If it is anything like this wonderful kitchen, I will be spending much time there with you."

They walked outside and, indeed, Beatrice was astounded at the large garden. It was neatly divided between herbs, vegetable plants and flowers. There were trellises and short fences to keep rabbits away. In one corner, there was a small shed for drying herbs and in another corner there was a bench to rest upon.

"It is lovely." Beatrice couldn't help the awe in her voice. "I have never seen a garden so perfect."

Molly's warm gaze met hers and, at once, Beatrice knew she'd found a good friend. "I was fearful that something was amiss with you not being present at the evening meal, Milady."

"Please, call me Beatrice. If you must use a title when around the others, I understand. But I prefer when in private, you refrain. I find it tiresome."

The woman smiled. "Very well, Beatrice. Can I ask

why you did not join the Lord last night?"

"He was cross with me." Beatrice pulled Molly to the bench. Once they sat, Beatrice told her of what happened in the forest. Molly laughed during most of the tale until having to wipe tears from her eyes.

"You are certainly the perfect match for our lord. However, I hate he was forced to punish you."

"My bum is, indeed, sore," Beatrice said and then let out a huff. "I find it intolerable that husbands can strike us as if we're children to be chastised."

Molly nodded. "Tis the way of our people. Not much can be done about it. I know the lord. He is not the kind to be cruel to women."

"Hmmm," Beatrice considered her husband. "I don't know him well enough to comment. However, I can tell you he could have used more force. I can sit without much bother."

Both laughed when Beatrice rocked side to side.

THE EVENING MEAL came too soon. Beatrice felt ill prepared to meet new people. However, it could not be postponed. That she'd missed the first meal could be excused due to travel, but a second day would bring unneeded speculation.

If the people suspected she'd been punished, they'd watch her like a hawk for any sign of discord between her and their lord.

Upon descending the stairs, Gavin escorted Beatrice to sit at a table at the front of the great room. It was new to her to sit at the high board. Yet, she was reassured with his presence next to her. Everyone in the room slid curious glances to her, most seeming friendly.

"How are you feeling?" Gavin asked as food was placed before them.

It was not a question she felt prepared to answer. Anger simmered. "Very well, thank you for asking. Being struck is a favorite pastime of mine," she replied with a forced smile for the sake of those who watched them.

His nostrils flared and jaw clenched. "I had no choice."

Sinclair cleared his throat and motioned to the tray of food. "I see Molly has outdone herself today."

Succulent meats upon the tray were accompanied with root vegetables. On another tray sat a variety of breads and cheeses. Everything invited a diner to eat with the wonderful aromas.

Gavin assisted in filling her plate before his own, waiting for their cups to be filled before standing. The room became instantly silent as everyone's attention moved to him.

"On this day, I declare a formal welcome to Hardigg Castle to my wife, Lady Beatrice, and her brother, Oscar Preston. With Lady Beatrice Mereworth at my side, we will ensure the strength and well-being of our people." He turned to her and nodded.

Everyone began calling out good wishes. An older man stood and held his arms up. "Your Grace, we wish you and Lady Beatrice many years and many children."

There were cheers of agreement and laughter.

"Lady Beatrice, I don't believe we've been formally introduced." The man she'd seen earlier sat on Gavin's right side. He leaned forward to speak to her. "I am Torquil Roberts, part of the duke's guard."

"And advisor," Gavin added, his eyes moving from the handsome man to her. "Torquil has been my closest friend for many years."

Sharp green eyes met hers. "Milady, at your service." His lips curved and he added. "I also echo the good wishes."

"Thank you." A warm flush climbed to her cheeks

at all the attention and her face began to ache from smiling at the crowd. Once everyone's attention was taken by the food, she was finally able to relax enough to eat.

Gavin studied her. "Tomorrow, the townspeople will come for a feast. The room will be filled to capacity. You must rest tonight."

She couldn't help but wonder if, once again, he'd wait until late to join her in bed.

TOO NERVOUS TO sleep, Beatrice paced before the fireplace, her tea cold and forgotten. Besides her duties to the home, she had to discuss with Molly what other tasks were expected of her.

Upon Lady Mereworth first marrying the Lord back at her village, Beatrice had heard she was often about, usually visiting townspeople or seeing about purchasing items at the market. It seemed strange to her that the lord's wife would shop as she had maids to do it for her. However, it must have been nice to see her doing so. However, once Lady Mereworth became reclusive, it had all stopped and she was not seen again.

Beatrice decided she'd do as the lady once did. She'd visit the people in their homes, purchase personal items for herself and Gavin in the village market as well as helping with the sick. Once that was settled in her mind, she wondered what to do about the current situation with her husband.

All through the evening meal, her husband remained distant. Although she was still angry with him, it was perplexing. A discussion was needed. No need to wait for him to decide when and how they'd relate to one another. In Beatrice's opinion, they'd become like Lord and Lady Mereworth the longer any distance between them remained.

Her stomach flipped when the door opened and Gavin appeared. His gaze met hers and he went directly to his wardrobe and began undressing. "How fare you, Beatrice?"

"Well, thank you. How about you?"

He pulled his tunic up over his head and turned to her. "I meant your bottom. Are you hurting?"

She jutted her chin out. "Do you ask again out of curiosity or because you care?"

"Come." Gavin held his hand out, waiting for her to decide whether to approach or not. Lips downturned and shoulders down, he appeared vulnerable. "Please."

Beatrice took his hand and he closed the distance between them drawing her close. The strength of Gavin's arms surrounded her and she inhaled the smell of him. He smelled of outdoors and heather. The fields surrounding the keep kept the air perfumed.

"I don't wish to strike you ever again. It sickened me." He pressed a kiss to her temple. "I was wrong to do it."

Finally, he said something she agreed with. However, she'd placed him in the difficult circumstance. How to agree with him without a promise not to disobey him in the future, she wasn't sure.

"I should not have done it. I realize it now. However, I did have good intentions."

Gavin let out a breath. "Would it be too much to expect you'll listen to me from now on?"

Did he truly expect her to reply to such a ridiculous thing? "I will endeavor to do my best to do as you ask."

He tilted her face up and his lips curved. "I suppose I have to accept that."

It was hard not to smile in return. She was glad to have gotten over the first problem together and relieved he'd initiated the conversation.

"How often will we..." she started, her eyes going

from his eyes to his lips. "Be intimate?"

"As often as you wish, dear one." He lifted her and carried her to the bed. "I am fortunate that you enjoyed it and look forward to us joining again."

"I do." Beatrice sighed when his mouth covered hers and Gavin began quick work of undressing them both.

Gavin did not stop until both were fully nude and then pulled her down to the edge of the bed until her legs dangled over the edge. "I will show you new things tonight, beauty."

In a trance, her eyes followed him as he bent and pressed his lips to her stomach. Her skin tingled in awareness as Gavin trailed his tongue to her side just above her pelvic bone. Swirling his tongue and mouth, he traced over her skin. Shots of heat sped to between her legs and she lifted her head.

His eyes met hers as he pulled her legs over his shoulders. "Relax. Allow me to bring you to release."

It was not easy to lie back not knowing exactly what he planned. When his warm mouth covered her sex, Beatrice jolted, unsure what to do.

His tongue slipped between her nether lips and she no longer cared. Heartbeats echoed and breathing came in gasps as Gavin continued the delicious torture. Lights spiraled as her eyelids fluttered. "Ah!" Beatrice cried out and bucked up into his mouth, wanting to tell him to stop, as she feared fainting yet at the same time to continue.

He blew a heated breath over her sex and then suckled the center into his mouth with so much force that Beatrice cried out and everything spiraled out of control.

While she floated in a daze of passion, Gavin thrust into her, stretching her until filling her deep and began moving in and out with long, leisurely strokes.

He pushed her legs up so her knees were spread and pressed down to hold her open as he moved faster. Once again, she climbed, the room disappearing. Beatrice could not keep from calling his name over and over again. The longer he continued, the more desperate she became for release. At the same time, the sensations were so wondrous she hoped they never stopped.

"Come with me, Beatrice."

She opened her eyes to see Gavin's face above her, his body taut and beautiful. Already darkened eyes looked almost black as he peered down at where they were joined. His hips continued in a steady rhythm and he released her right leg to touch her center. It only took three strokes to bring her to a release so hard, she screamed.

When Gavin collapsed over her, he shuddered and thrust twice more, his heated seed spilling.

Beatrice could not gather her wits. Like a rag doll, her limbs were useless as her husband, lifted and settled her upon the pillow.

Contentment like no other filled her when Gavin gathered her close.

They lay together in silence while the night sounds serenaded outside the window. It was early still, Beatrice mused. She'd expected to have tea and discuss her responsibilities. After the discussion about their relationship, of course.

"Gavin?"

"Mmmm?"

"I wish to know what you expect of me on a daily basis. Can I go to the market and such?" Her words slurred as sleep threatened to take over.

"Is this what you wish to speak of right now?"

Beatrice pondered, her fingers tracing over his chest. "What else can we talk about?"

His chuckle was deep. "I could show you more ways to make love."

The idea had merit. However, she wasn't sure of her ability to muster any strength at the moment. "I don't think I could do much more than be still for the lesson at this moment."

"How do you feel about what I did between your legs?"

The question caught her off guard. Beatrice pondered. "I enjoyed it quite a lot."

"You can do the same for me." He left the sentence hanging in silence.

"Do you want me to do it now?"

"No beauty. You are tired. We'll leave it for another night."

Curious, she pictured his staff and how it was possible to give him pleasure in such a way. A thought occurred. Molly was married. She'd ask her and surprise him.

"Gavin?"

"Mmmm?"

"What is your full name?"

Once again, he chuckled and yawned. "My name is Gavin Alexander Tavish Mereworth."

"I've never liked the name Tavish," she replied, barely able to keep her eyes open. "It reminds me of old man Tavish who used to beg for coin while trying to look under our skirts when mother and I walked to the market."

"Perhaps I should change my name. Although I do like the idea of looking under your skirt."

Beatrice giggled. "You may keep the name."

When she was about to ask him about Torquil, a soft snore broke the silence of the room. Beatrice smiled and studied Gavin's profile.

He was, indeed, handsome and a good man. Although she didn't know her husband well, she knew, somehow, it was inevitable that she'd fall in love with him. The thought shook her to alertness. If she loved him and he never loved her in return, how would it feel?

Someday, she hoped to have his children. She and Gavin would grow old together and live at Hardigg Castle for the rest of their lives. It was her deepest hope they did fall in love. She wasn't so innocent to believe it would happen just because of a wish. It wasn't always the case for marriages. But for her and Gavin, it was Beatrice's genuine desire.

# CHAPTER ELEVEN

G AVIN STROLLED WITH a farmer on one side and Torquil on the other as he listened to the farmer's complaints. It was the same one he'd heard from others. Someone from the neighboring Lord's township had trespassed onto Mereworth lands. A few of his sheep were stolen and they'd accosted this man's daughter. Although the lass proclaimed she was not hurt, Gavin could tell the father did not believe she'd been left untouched.

"We should visit Lord Roberts," Torquil said. "There is no need for further action on our part until we ask him first for recompense of some sort." His green eyes went to the harried farmer. "Unfortunately, there are things that cannot be rectified. Would you agree to the scoundrel marrying your daughter?"

"A Roberts?" The farmer's alarmed exclamation was accompanied with bulging eyes. "Never."

Torquil nodded.

"I beg your pardon, sir," the farmer stuttered. "I know you are from that family. But we do not consider you to be…" At a loss for words, the man left the sentence dangling.

"No need to explain," Torquil replied.

They mounted and Gavin studied his friend for a moment. "Do you think your father will want to hear anything we have to say? You left your home over ten years ago. They no longer consider you a Roberts."

His friend scanned the area, a habit to always be on guard. "I know. Sometimes I barely remember my life there. However, even if they consider me a Mereworth, they must explain to me the why of their actions. They have no need of anything."

"Your father is not a fair man, Torquil. You know that more than most. Perhaps his people are in need. Hungry."

Torquil turned to a guard. "Go ahead to the keep. I will require a guard of twenty to travel to my father's estate.

Gavin considered accompanying him, but he knew any suggestion to it would be rebuffed. Relations between the two families had barely settled. There was no need to start up another war because of one young woman and some sheep. He considered the young woman. She was, no doubt, attempting to keep her father from getting himself killed. However, if she became with child, the consequences could be dire.

UPON ENTERING THE castle walls, Gavin guided his horse toward the stables. Beyond them, the archers were lined up loosing arrows at targets.

Amongst them was Beatrice.

He'd not spoken to her about hunting as yet. She would never be allowed to do so. The lass had been wise enough not to mention it, especially after the debacle when traveling there.

Beatrice was an amazing markswoman, her shot clean and precise. However, she was no match in strength to his archers who ribbed her about the depth of her arrows. Gavin's eyes widened when she kicked one in the shin and the man hopped up on one leg cursing.

He waited to see what would happen next. The archer hobbled to her and, with squared shoulders, pointed at a target. They took several paces backward and lifted bows.

From where he stood, Gavin could not see how

well the targets were hit. Beatrice and the archer moved forward as a unit while talking. Finally, near the targets, his wife's shoulders fell. She nodded at whatever the archer said and they shook hands.

Interesting.

Afterwards, she shrugged at whatever the man said and both laughed. Still smiling, she looked to where Gavin stood and her eyes widened. No doubt, she'd been told Gavin would be gone all day and she didn't expect to get caught with her bow and arrows so soon after being punished.

Beatrice hurried toward him. "Your archer, Craig, is a great marksman." Her eyes moved side-to-side and pearly teeth sunk into the corner of her bottom lip. "I was just checking the weather."

What could he say to her? There was much to learn about the feisty lass. As Lord and husband, his roles became complicated when dealing with Beatrice.

"It is unusual for the lord's wife to practice with the guard. I can have a target set up for you near the gardens."

Her brows fell and her lips thinned. "Why?"

"You could get hurt out there," he motioned to the guard's area where two men sparred with swords.

"Beatrice, why am I pointing out the obvious to you?"

"I am not so daft to get in the way of men involved in swordplay. I do find it insulting that you think me to be so."

Gavin stalked toward the gardens. "I will show you where it is safer. I don't wish to argue."

"I don't wish to be treated like a child."

"Then stop behaving like one."

They faced off, both with clenched jaws and glares directed at one another.

Why did the woman have to try him so? It became a battle of wills. He'd not give in to her regardless of whether it was important or not. It was her safety he was concerned for.

Beatrice hunched forward. "I tire of being treated as if I cannot think for myself."

"I tire of you proving it to be true."

"Good afternoon to the newly married lovers." Sinclair appeared between them. He maintained a wide smile and placed his hands on their shoulders. "Everyone is watching. I suggest you kiss her, Gavin. Or laugh as if you were both playacting. Do something."

Beatrice's eyes widened and she slid a look to a

group of women who didn't pretend not to be staring. She allowed her head to fall back and laughed. "Your brother is a selfish oaf."

"My new wife is a spoiled chit," Gavin replied and leaned forward to kiss her curved lips.

He took a step back, afraid she'd kick him or swing her bow. "I must go deal with other matters." He turned and walked away.

Gavin doubted the people were fooled. However, he'd ensure at the feast that night they behaved as if unable to keep from each other. In truth, at the moment, he'd pictured hanging his wife on a peg in the cloakroom until he could better deal with her.

Seated in the great room, Gavin let out a sigh as his gaze traveled over the people assembled. His towns-people needed him.

The day droned on, one family after the other appearing with need of his counsel or to arbitrate a disagreement. Ironic, since he needed the same thing when dealing with his own wife.

"YOU SHOULD BE in there with your husband." Molly sat beside Beatrice in the kitchen. "It shows the people solidarity between you and the lord."

Beatrice let out a sigh. "I will go there now. Although I do believe Gavin dislikes me."

The kitchen was the most comfortable place for Beatrice. There with Molly, she could assist, request guidance and never felt awkward. Anytime she was around Gavin or any of his people, judgment was aimed at her from every direction, it seemed.

The cook stirred a large pot. "I sincerely doubt it, Beatrice. I believe he is quite taken by you."

"Physically, yes. But our personalities are so different. I am forever doing what he considers unbecoming of a lady."

Molly laughed. "Like insisting I call you Beatrice, Milady?"

"I want to be friends. I don't want close friends to call me by a title."

"Understandable. However, you must assert yourself before the people. Stand by their lord, support him and do as he asks. If you show lack of respect for him, what message does that send the people?"

At once, Beatrice felt horrible. Once again, she'd embarrassed Gavin. "I don't know why he chose to marry me." She let out a long sigh and hunched forward. "I was meant to marry a daft, brawny goat herder."

Their laughter rung out and Molly pulled Beatrice to stand. "Go now. See about your duties."

EVERY FACE TURNED to her as she walked to sit next to Gavin. She placed a filled tankard at his right elbow and settled into the chair, her chin lifted just right and a soft smile on her lips.

Gavin leaned over. "Should I be worried, dear wife?"

"Not at all. I am here to learn. If that is acceptable?" She batted her lashes and his eyes widened just enough.

"Of course."

Immediately, Beatrice became lost in the many requests, pledges and introductions Gavin oversaw without seeming to tire. After an hour, she wondered how he remained so composed as two men hollered over one another over whether or not a young girl had agreed to marry one or the other first. The girl in question stood by with a finger on her lips as if enjoying the spectacle.

"What do you think?" Gavin surprised Beatrice by asking. "Who deserves to win the girl?"

Beatrice studied the young girl. "Neither. She is

playing a game. Promised them both the same thing for attention. I believe it would serve her well to see them promised to others."

Her husband's eyebrows rose. "Like whom?"

"Those sisters over there with the beautiful red hair. They are both studying the men with admiration."

Gavin held a hand up and the men quieted, but continued glaring at one another. "Gilbert, come forward." He motioned to an older man who stood beside the red-haired beauties. "Did you not come requesting proper husbands for your daughters?"

The ruddy man with the same hued hair as the young girls grinned. "Aye, Your Grace, I do."

"Very well," Gavin looked to the now frozen duo, who'd been arguing. "I do believe these two are available. Donald and Edward, I believe it's best for you to be married off to others. This way the contest between you will end." He looked to the now wide-eyed girls. "Anna and Flora, come forth to be betrothed."

Immediately, the four affected people began a study of each other and within moments, paired off and stood before Gavin. It seemed the girl the men had been arguing about was forgotten by young men, who were now obviously thrilled at the prospect of such beautiful brides.

Gavin motioned for the clergyman to come forth and formalize the betrothal. Meanwhile, the girl the men had been fighting over fled from the room, wailing.

"How do you remember everyone's name?" Beatrice asked her husband while the clergyman rambled on about purity and such nonsense.

By the way the newly betrothed couples kept stealing glances at each other, it would be a miracle if the young women would arrive as maidens on their wedding days.

"The most important thing about a person is the name they go by. I make it a practice to memorize every one of my people's names. Although it's a difficult task at times, my father impressed upon me the importance of it. And I agree."

Beatrice continued to be impressed by Gavin's ability to govern over the people. He was firm but fair. Yet at times, he laughed at strange requests until even the silly person joined in.

Finally, it was announced that everyone should

depart so the great hall could be prepared for the great feast to be held within hours.

"I don't know how you can possibly plan for a day of festivities after all this." Beatrice stood and stretched. "I must speak to Molly. She didn't seem too concerned with the amount of food to be prepared."

"Most of it is being prepared by the women of the village. Although the feasting will be grand, every family will bring food to share. It's the way we've always done it. There are two large boars being roasted by a group of men and once Torquil returns from his duties, he and the rest of the guard will see about setting tables out in the courtyard for those who do not fit in here."

He took her hand and lifted it to his lips. "Thank you."

"For what?" Beatrice wasn't sure what he could be grateful for.

"Being here next to me. I know we had a disagreement earlier. It is probable we will have many more given the difference in our temperaments. However, it is refreshing to see you do not hold grudges."

"Is that what you think?" She narrowed her eyes, but smiled to let him know she teased.

"Honestly, I am not sure." He turned away as the future brides' father neared to speak to him.

Beatrice retraced her steps to the kitchen. Upon hearing her name, she slowed when nearing the study.

"She is very stubborn. I am not sure it's best for her to know. Gavin has enough to handle without her knowing she must produce two heirs in quick succession." Oscar sounded annoyed, perhaps frustrated.

Sinclair grunted. "However, if they argue, I am not sure how often they will join. He's been instructed to bed her every night except during her monthly courses, of course."

"It will happen. I am sure of it. Once the first child arrives, and she heals, they can continue to join until she is with a second child. Once two boys are born, Gavin's duty will be fulfilled."

Sinclair chuckled. "After, they can join for sport."

Moving quickly, she hurried to the kitchen and sunk into a chair. Gavin had married her to be a brooding mare for heirs. The men spoke of her as if she were nothing more than a cow, needed only to give birth to sons. Heaviness fell over her chest as if someone placed a huge stone upon it. Any feelings she hoped Gavin had were nonexistent.

He'd spoken to her brother and his about how often they joined. She couldn't process what to do. In all honesty, it was an impossible situation. If she were to be honest, it was what the Lord married for. To ensure his title be passed along, the seat of governing the people. In Gavin's case, he had the added responsibility of a dukedom to pass.

When Molly entered, Beatrice lifted her head and sat straighter. Her eyes flat, she scanned the counters. "Is everything ready for the feast?"

"Aye," Molly replied with an inquisitive look, but she didn't say more.

"Very well. See that the maids fill all the pitchers and ensure enough trays are filled with trenchers."

"Yes Milady," Molly used her title noting the change in her countenance. Several maids rushed in and stood before Beatrice. "Instruct the lads and the chambermaids to see about replacing the rushes in the great room and scrubbing all the tabletops. Hurry, go."

Beatrice left the kitchen and walked past the great room toward the stairs. Gavin caught up with her. "Will you rest before changing?"

"Yes. Unless there is anything else you require."

"No...nothing." Gavin took her elbow and walked

with her to the bottom of the stairs. "Rest well."

Beatrice gave him a curt nod and went up to the privacy of the chamber where tears immediately flowed.


Music from traveling bards flowed over the constant conversations and the clinking of dishes. Loud calls for toasts from different men constantly interrupted Gavin and Beatrice's meal, but he didn't mind. It was satisfying to see approval of his choice of wife by his household.

Each time the crowd called for a kiss, Beatrice's lips would purse and she'd lean forward accepting his press of lips. Although she maintained a soft curve to her lips and was attentive to all who approached, he sensed something different about her.

When a maid neared, Beatrice snapped her fingers and chastised the girl, telling her to stand straighter. After a puzzled look, the maid hurried away, albeit straighter.

"Are you enjoying yourself?" Gavin leaned into her ear.

Her flat eyes met his. "Of course. Why would I not?"

Sinclair neared and scanned the room. "Have you spoken to Torquil yet?"

"No. He and the guard arrived just a few minutes ago." His advisor had yet to enter the room. However, Oscar had and the other guardsmen ate at one of the tables.

"Is something amiss?" Sinclair studied him for a moment before looking to Beatrice. She was speaking to a woman holding a small child. "I have to admit to be surprised at your wife's good behavior tonight. It's almost like someone else."

That was it. Someone or something had happened and changed her. "Why do you say that?" Gavin hoped Sinclair would give him some insight.

"Although I know she was well raised, today is the first time I've seen her so composed, so calm."

Indeed, she was calm. Almost to the point it was surreal. Her movements measured, every expression no matter how pleasant did not affect the flatness in her gaze. Perhaps, she'd drunk too much mead?

IT WAS LATE that evening when he finally led her from the room. Her gaze barely flickered over his as she allowed Grisilda to help her undress. Unlike most nights when the two would chatter about inconsequential things, this night she asked the maid to leave as soon as her gown was removed. "You may go, Grisilda. I will see about my hair."

On the way out, Grisilda gave him a questioning look. Gavin shrugged in response.

"Beatrice. Is there something you wish to discuss with me? We argued earlier about your archery practice. Is that what has you so distant?"

"Distant?" Her chuckle crackled with lack of mirth. "I cannot be angry when you are correct. My behavior up until this point has been horrendous. I will no longer use the bow and arrow. Nor do I wish to go hunting or any such thing." She pulled the brush through her hair and the waves fell down past her shoulders.

"I didn't say you could no longer use your bow."

Her shoulders lifted and fell. "Nonetheless, I understand my place. I am to be available to you, body, mind and soul at all times. Especially my body until I produce heirs."

*She knew.*

Gavin swallowed, not sure what to say. Many thoughts occurred. He should have told her right away.

Explained the danger of losing his title and why it mattered. Now anything he said could be held against him by her as a way to justify his actions.

"Is that what you think I want?" Stupid question. Not sure why it came out of his mouth, Gavin clenched his jaw.

Without hesitating her brushing, she shook her head. "I don't think anything. I know what I am to do and that is all that matters."

Gavin walked to her and placed a hand on her shoulder. Beatrice stiffened, then relaxed. "I will explain things to you. It will be up to you what you think of it."

Jumping to her feet, she moved around him to the bed. It was hard to be fascinated when she pushed the chemise off her shoulders and allowed it to pool around her feet. "We need to join before it gets much later. I am quite exhausted."

When he looked from her feet to her face, she didn't shift, although he did notice a slight hitch to her breathing. Beatrice was not indifferent to him. However, at the moment, her feelings were hurt.

Gavin pulled his shirt off and removed his britches, allowing them to fall where he stood. Then, he approached his wife, scooped her up in his arms and carried her to the bed.

Lying on his side, he held her flush against him and covered her mouth with his. The thudding of his heart and immediate arousal did not matter. What did matter was reassuring his fiery bride. He had to keep demonstrating to her that she had options. He'd never taken a woman without knowing she wanted him as much and Gavin wasn't about to start with Beatrice.

She trembled when he slid his palms down her back and cupped her round bottom.

"I admire your inner strength," Gavin whispered in her ear. "It is only when you want me that we will join. Whether once a day or once a week, it has to be by mutual agreement. Never will I mandate you give yourself to me. My body is yours, Beatrice. But only when you wish it."

Gavin wrapped his arms around her and nuzzled at the apex between her neck and shoulders. "Now rest, beauty. We will talk more about this. I hope once I explain, you will understand."

After a shuddering breath, Beatrice finally lifted her face up and searched his as if ensuring he spoke the truth. She nodded and pressed her forehead into his chest.

In that moment, Gavin knew he would do anything to protect her. Give his life for the beauty in his arms. He was falling in love with his wife.

"Tomorrow, we will talk." Once again, Gavin kissed her temple and allowed slumber to overtake him.

# CHAPTER TWELVE

B EATRICE WAS SURPRISED to wake with Gavin still in the bed. The day prior must have taken a toll on him. She'd never considered how much work was upon his shoulders. Between visiting the surrounding lands, overseeing disputes and requests, then having to entertain late into the evening, he did more than most could accomplish daily.

When he stirred, she watched, mesmerized as his eyelids fluttered. Gavin's lips curved when noting her regard. "You're awake." The comment was raspy with sleep. Then his brow furrowed. "Why hasn't anyone woken me?" He looked to the door.

"Everyone is tired after a long day. The castle is quiet still."

He pulled her against him. "We have to see about the departure of our guests. Some left early, I'm willing to bet. They have farms to tend to."

Having a conversation with Gavin while remaining

in bed was how she would love to start each day. Beatrice bit her lip. "I do believe some of the women are expecting tea with me. So I will be busy for a while today."

With his fingertips, he tilted her chin up. "You are a wonderful wife to entertain the lot of them." His mouth covered hers before she could reply. The longer his kiss lingered the harder it was to keep from pressing against him.

Moments later, unable to keep from it, Beatrice took Gavin by the hip and pulled him against her. She wanted nothing more at the moment than to join with him, not because she had to, but because she chose to.

Already aroused, his hard sex slid between her legs, the skin silky against her own. He thrust forward and moaned in her ear. The alluring gruff moans were almost her undoing.

Finally, he pulled her leg over his hip and guided himself into her. Both let out a loud sound of satisfaction when he plunged deep.

They made love in a lazy fashion, mouths tasting while their bodies rocked in and out until both lost control. Gavin grunted into her hair as he released into her already spent body.

"MILADY, I LOOK forward to your visits," the healer woman said. So far, the townswomen had been friendly and quite lovely to Beatrice.

"I plan to do so regularly. My mother tutored me in healing and herbs. I would gladly help out when possible."

As everyone left, a pretty but somber woman lingered behind. "I hear you and the Lord may not be compatible. That you argue constantly. Is it true, Milady?"

The question was not out of concern, but because the woman wanted fodder for gossip. Beatrice chuckled softly. "Don't tell anyone." She made a show out of glancing to the other women who walked ahead and then whispered. "Our heated disputes are kindling for a different type of exchange later…in private." She waved her hand in the air. "Sometimes we get carried away and forget where we are when sparring." A long sigh escaped at remembering their lovemaking just that morning.

The young woman's eyes widened and then she nodded. "I am glad to hear it, Milady." From the downturn of her lips, she was not.

ONCE THE WOMEN left, Beatrice dawdled in the kitchen for a bit, but was sent out by Molly when she'd offered to help. In the great room, the maids and young lads cleaned up, the women moved about while chatting about the festivities. They stopped when Beatrice entered. "Is there something we can do for you, Milady?" one of the women called out to her.

"No, please continue." She went to the stairs and climbed to her chamber to find Grisilda cleaning there. "Grisilda, I apologize for how I spoke to you last night."

Her friend smiled and let out a breath. "Oh, thank goodness. I was scared you'd decided to change how we would regard each other from now on."

Beatrice took Grisilda's hands and led her to the chairs in front of the fireplace. "I feel lost in this new world. I don't know what my place is. What my function is."

"To oversee the household, of course. Go over meal plans with Molly, see about the gardens, lists for the market, visit the villagers, and see about your husband. There is so much to do, Beatrice."

There was a lot to be done. But it seemed it was all accomplished without her help. "It took but a few moments to ensure all was well."

Grisilda giggled. "You are not used to being in this elevated position. Perhaps you should ask His Grace to allow a visit to a neighboring Lord and meet with his wife."

"No, I can't. The only nearby Lord is Lord Roberts and they are not on good terms with us." She pressed her lips together. "It is almost two days ride to visit De Wolfe and his wife."

"Perhaps if you visit Lady Roberts and the wives get along, it would make for a better situation."

Beatrice's mouth fell open. "What a grand idea." She hugged Grisilda. "Thank you. You will go with me, of course."

The maid stood and went back to shaking out the bedding. "Of course."

TORQUIL STOOD NEXT to the sideboard holding a cup. Whether ale or tea, Gavin wasn't sure. "My father sends his congratulations on your marriage."

"So I take it you had a civil conversation?"

His friend pressed his lips together and frowned. "Civil with bitter undertones. However, he did promise to speak to his people about trespassing. Also, he wants to make amends by offering that if the farmer's daughter will name the man who accosted her, he will agree to a marriage or recompense of their choice."

"Interesting." Gavin drank his tea. "Did he ask you to return?"

"He suggested it by implying I'd receive land." This time Torquil gulped from the cup and grimaced. *Whiskey.*

Although the past tore the father and illegitimate son apart, Gavin never questioned Torquil's fidelity to him. Whatever Torquil decided, the man would remain a close friend. He waited to see if Torquil would elaborate.

"I can't return. Each time I go there I find my stomach churning."

When Torquil was but ten and six, he'd been betrothed to a beautiful young girl named Ellen. Without reason, his father had the betrothal undone. Then months later, he married the girl himself. Now, years later, they remained married with sons and daughters. Although Ellen was quite sweet, she'd never given any indication of being heartbroken over Torquil.

His friend, however, never forgave his father. He'd been madly fascinated with Ellen and had proclaimed his love for her publicly. To have Ellen, as his father's bride was not only humiliating for the younger Torquil, but also it had broken the young man's heart.

"Do you still love her?" Gavin wasn't sure why he asked. Finding he was currently losing his heart, fear of what would happen if Beatrice ever broke his own heart had begun to take hold.

"No. I don't believe I ever did. Not really. Perhaps the young naïve me did, but no, not any longer. However, I cannot understand why my father would do this to his own son. Being bastard born, I never had aspiration to gain much. Ellen, however, was my one treasure."

Understanding now, Gavin nodded. "I believe if the same happened to me, I would also leave my home."

"There is another matter we must speak of…" they began to discuss duties, giving Gavin a reprieve from wondering about Beatrice and what she was doing at the moment.

"How far is it to the Roberts' home?" Beatrice asked her husband later. "I wish to visit the Lady Roberts."

"No." In Gavin's study, the word hung in the air between them. "It would be dangerous to send my wife to the Roberts' territory. Our relationship is not strong as yet."

"That is why I think it would be a good idea for his wife and me to get to know each other. Have you met her? We could invite them here."

Her husband's gaze met hers. He let out a sigh and looked to the doorway. "She's lovely and seems a good person." He stood and went to the door then returned and sat next to her. "I will tell you about her…"

Moments later, Beatrice frowned. "I see how her coming here would be discomfiting to Torquil. However, keeping our people safe is more important is it not?"

"I agree with your wife," Torquil said as he entered the room. Beatrice wanted to kick herself for her inability to keep her voice down.

Although he stood proud, a warrior through and through, there was just a flicker of vulnerability in his eyes. "Lady Beatrice. It is a good idea to build trust between the families. For many years, there has been strife and too many lives lost over unimportant things."

Gavin's lips curved, pride expanding his chest. "I made a good decision in choosing you for my partner.

Not only a beauty, but intelligent as well."

Soft warmth filled her and she smiled at the men in the room. Soon, she'd get to know Torquil better.

There was a quiet strength about the warrior that she liked. Perhaps, he'd be best married and settled. It would help Torquil to better deal with Ellen's visits if he were settled. Beatrice decided to discuss the matter with Gavin later.

It was important that they build better relations with the Roberts.

"What are you thinking?" Torquil narrowed his eyes. "You look to me as if mentally measuring me for a tunic."

Gavin's eyebrows lifted. "Is something amiss, Beatrice?"

She ignored Gavin and looked up at Torquil. "Why aren't you married and with young yet?"

It was comical to see the usually composed man's mouth open and close. He blinked and then frowned. "I have not been inclined to."

"Time passes quickly. How old are you? Five and thirty? Soon, you'll be much too old to sire."

"Beatrice," Gavin said with a tinge of warning although his lips quivered in an attempt not to smile.

Torquil let out a breath. "Why would you have me married off? Afraid I'll steal my father's bride back? I have no intention of doing so."

"No," Beatrice said. "I don't sense you do. However, I do think every man needs a wife to settle him."

"You didn't wish to marry," Gavin, the annoying man, spouted. "Why do you champion marriage now?"

Beatrice looked to him from the side of her eyes. "It's different for a woman. We don't need settling."

"Hmmm." Thankfully, her husband didn't elaborate on his thoughts. It would not do for him to point out she was quiet wild and unsettled even then.

Torquil lifted his eyes to the ceiling. "I do not wish to marry anytime soon, Lady Beatrice. I do, however, wish to discuss the guard's duties with His Grace."

"I will leave you to that then." Beatrice stood and then leaned to press a kiss to Gavin's lips. "Discuss inviting the Roberts," she whispered, knowing Torquil could hear.

From the study, she made her way to the kitchens where she found Molly sitting down to a cup of tea. "Milady, I'll fix you one." She started to stand, but Beatrice pushed her shoulder to keep her in place.

"No, don't. I'm not in the mood for tea at the moment." She plopped down in a chair without care and Molly shook her head and smiled.

"I need to ask you about something." Beatrice scanned the room to ensure it was empty. "It's about bedsport."

Molly chuckled. "Very well. What perplexes you?"

"How can a woman please a man with her mouth?"

Molly spit out her tea and coughed violently. Beatrice jumped up and banged her on the back. "Oh, that was not the question I expected," Molly, sputtered between coughs and laughter. Tears ran down her face and she wiped them away with her apron. "Goodness, you surprised me."

Moments later they sat at the table with a thick carrot between them. Molly kept watch while Beatrice practiced placing the thick end of the carrot into her mouth. Most of the time, they laughed too much to accomplish any kind of training.

"Oh, His Grace comes." Molly yanked the carrot from Beatrice and took a healthy bite out of the tip.

Beatrice couldn't help but burst out laughing just as Gavin stepped in. His eyes went from Molly, who tried to look serious as she stood with a carrot in her hand while chewing, to Beatrice, who fought valiantly to keep from giggling.

His eyes narrowed and scanned the room. "I came to ask if you'd like to walk about the garden."

"That would be lovely." Beatrice stood and a second carrot rolled onto the floor. She'd forgotten about the carrot they'd deemed too small compared to Gavin's sex.

It rolled across the floor and Molly dissolved into fits of laughter, collapsing on the chair. "I…I…apologize…y-y-your Grace."

The poor woman couldn't stop, so Beatrice grabbed Gavin's hand and pulled him to the door.

Once outside, she walked alongside him with a wide smile on her face.

"What were you two doing?" Gavin asked. "I feel as if I interrupted some sort of mischief."

"Nothing like that. Molly was teaching me about gardening."

"I see."

They walked to the edge of the gardens where a solitary bench under a trellis burdened with ivy provided both privacy and shade. Beatrice looked behind them, noting the short wall and the building's wall did make the spot perfect for a tryst.

"This seems a place a young man would bring a lass and steal a kiss."

Gavin's lips curved. "Aye. However, it also is the perfect place to have a conversation without fear of being overheard."

So he planned to speak. Beatrice attempted without much success to draw her mind away from what she'd rather be doing.

"Beatrice. I appreciate your dedication to our people. It makes me happy to know you already care enough to work towards bringing better relations between the Roberts and us. Your idea, although it has merit, will have to wait. It is still too soon. I fear a disaster by bringing those who have killed our people into their midst. The Roberts, as well, will have similar situations, I'm sure. Just earlier this year, there were deaths on both sides."

Beatrice nodded and led him to the bench where she lowered to sit while he stood. Her lips curved at finding herself at the perfect height, parallel to his midsection.

"As the years pass," he continued, "once more time goes by, the freshness of anger and resentment will fade. Wounds will heal. Then we can consider... what are you doing?"

She pulled his tunic up and pulled his britches down to his hips. She peered between his legs. He was flaccid, but no matter. Molly said all she had to do was take it in hand.

"Beatrice?" Gavin stopped speaking when she gripped his staff and stroked it. He looked over his shoulder. "Here?"

"Be still," she said concentrating on getting him hard so she could do as she'd practiced. "I want to show you something."

"Ah…" Hardening followed his sharp intake of breath and several hitched breaths as she stroked him several more times.

With measure, she took his upper thigh and pulled him closer. Then just as she'd practiced, she licked the rim of his staff with her tongue flat. After a few times, she slowly pulled him into her mouth until he hit the back of her throat. She repeated the movement, mimicking lovemaking several times, then allowed him almost fully out of her mouth and suckled the tip.

She looked up to see him looking down with fascination, neck muscles taut, nostrils flared. Happiness surged that he enjoyed it.

Once again, she took him fully into her mouth, sucking while stroking him with her hand until he grabbed her head and began thrusting. Aroused, she fought to breathe, but she relaxed her throat enough to allow the fast penetrations.

"Ah!" Gavin pulled out and spilled onto the ground, his arms resting on the back of the bench keeping her trapped as his chest heaved.

Leaning forward, he kissed her, his mouth ravishing her lips as if a hungry man possessed. Beatrice fell backward onto the bench and he followed, covering her with his large bulk.

It would have been uncomfortable if not for the need to have him. When his hand found her core and he began stroking her, pushing a finger into her while the other slid between her sex, she became undone within moments.

SOMETIME LATER, THEY walked back to the front of the keep. Beatrice glanced at her husband. His lips curved with satisfaction at having brought her to culmination more than once. "I am not sure the walk in the garden should always end as today." She mocked him. "What would people think?"

"They will think their Lord is a very lucky man, indeed."

Beatrice laughed.

"Your Grace. A messenger has arrived." A guard met them at the door. "From the Duke of Aldorf."

# CHAPTER THIRTEEN

**W**HEN THEY ENTERED the great room, Torquil, Sinclair and Oscar were already positioned to flank him. The intimidating lineup before him, the messenger had beads of sweat forming on his brow and upper lip as his rounded eyes followed Gavin who came to stand between his brother and Oscar.

Unfortunately, just as tall and broad as the others, it made the poor messenger's eyes grow larger. "My Lord," the messenger lowered his head.

"Tell me your message." Gavin spoke, keeping his voice level as a trickle of apprehension traveled down his spine. Whatever was Aldorf up to now?

The messenger cleared his throat. "His Grace sends his good wishes and congratulations on the occasion of your marriage. He wishes to inform you his brother has been bestowed the title of Duke of Elshire." The messenger took a breath. "He also wishes to invite you to attend the celebration ball a fortnight hence."

"So he is informing us that he is no longer a threat to our lord's title?" Torquil asked the messenger, who stood rigid. "You did not address him properly."

"I-I apologize, Your Grace." Once again, the messenger bowed his head. "I am rather nervous, you see."

Gavin gave Torquil a dull glance. "Very well, messenger. Remain through tomorrow. Sup with us this evening. I will give you a message for the duke in the morning."

Properly dismissed, the young man practically sprinted from the room.

"Where do you think he goes?" Sinclair asked, watching the messenger disappear.

"Probably to piss and then to ask the guards where he can lay down and get over his nerves."

"Should we send him some herbs to sniff?" Oscar asked, chuckling.

Beatrice, who'd remained silent and sat at one of the tables, shook her head. "You scared him witless." She looked to Gavin. "What will you reply?"

He could see she was considering the possibilities of attending an elegant affair. Women tended to see the more subtle side of things. Dresses, music and such. While he had to confer with Sinclair and Torquil and decide what the true reason behind the invitation was.

"I<small>T WOULD BEHOOVE</small> you for Beatrice to be with child by the time of the ball," Torquil said later as they remained in the great room alone now. "Perhaps, send our own messenger informing him of why she can't travel."

"Would it be a good idea for me to attend alone then?" Gavin asked.

Oscar leaned forward. "It would be a perfect occasion to be killed with hopes Beatrice gives birth to a girl."

"It's not the title Aldorf lusts after. It's the fact that you were titled and he is not the only one in Cumbria with power. You have vast lands, faithful people and are well liked."

"Jealousy? I doubt it. De Wolfe, has a larger stronghold on the area than I." Gavin threw his hands up. "I wish to live in peace and take care of my people. Men like Aldorf, who live a life of leisure off the work of those they govern, are an annoyance. If anyone should be killed…" he left the sentence hanging.

"Truer words are not spoken," Torquil said. "However, we must proceed with delicacy. Not attending without a good reason would look badly upon you. Attending alone, although dangerous, could be a better option. Sinclair and I can go with you while Oscar and the guard watch over the keep."

Oscar looked to Torquil. "I am not sure I'll be accepted as a leader yet. I have only arrived."

"The guards see your strength and know you are loyal as your sister married our lord. They already respect you." Torquil left no room for argument. "Now let's discuss what we should do."

THROUGHOUT THE EVENING meal, Beatrice kept stealing glances at her husband. Brow crinkled, he was distracted. He barely touched his food as he scanned the room constantly.

"Is something wrong?" she whispered into this ear.

"I am not sure," he replied and then leaned away. "Where is the messenger?" he asked Torquil, who also began to look over the people in attendance.

The warrior stood and left. Moments later, several of the guard followed him out.

"Do you think he left?" Beatrice looked to Gavin. "Quite strange, don't you think?"

A short time later, Torquil returned and leaned

into Gavin. "He's dead. I believe he killed himself. In his hand was a dagger used to cut open his own throat."

Beatrice swallowed. "Why?"

"To make it look as if we did it." Gavin stood and motioned Torquil to follow. Several people in the room took notice, but returned to eating. The only ones who did not were several of the guard who stood and followed their Lord out.

Alone at the high board, Beatrice studied her food unsure of what to do next. Finally, she motioned Grisilda over. The young girl normally ate at one of the tables with some of the village girls.

"What happens?" Grisilda sat gingerly when Beatrice yanked her arm to pull her down. "I am not sure I should sit here."

"Hush. Tell me. Did anyone see the messenger today after he left the great room?"

Grisilda shrugged. "I saw him speaking to one of the guardsmen, Liam, the red-haired one. Then later, he was getting water from the well. I figured he was going to bathe before eating."

Interesting. "Did you or any of the maids speak to him?"

"I do believe he asked for soap and cloths from the stable hands."

"I see." Beatrice got up. "Come with me."

It made no sense that if a man planned to kill himself, he would wash up beforehand. Not only that, why would the young man agree to such a thing? She supposed under threat that people could be driven to almost anything.

Outside, the guard stood in two lines as Gavin spoke. Liam stood on the end, his gaze moving from Gavin to Oscar before narrowing.

Beatrice took Grisilda's hand and pulled her toward the stable. Inside, the older man who watched over the horses greeted them with a cheerful wave. "Good eve, Milady, what brings you to my humble stables?"

"I have a question for you," Beatrice said and neared the man. He nodded in agreement.

"Of course."

"Did you speak to the messenger?"

"Aye, Milady, I did. Quite a nice lad. He asked for soap and cloths so he could wash up for the evening meal."

"Did he say when he planned to return?"

"Yes, Milady. He said on the morrow. He was anxious, as he was nervous about Liam. The man enjoys intimidating others."

"I see. Thank you." Beatrice let out a breath. "The messenger is dead."

The old man crossed himself. "Too bad. He was a nice young lad."

They walked back to the courtyard and she motioned Gavin over. Sinclair followed him, while Torquil and Oscar continued speaking to the guard.

"The messenger did not kill himself. He was killed." Beatrice looked from one brother to the other and explained everything she'd learned.

"It makes little sense," Sinclair said in a low tone lest they be heard. "Why would Liam or anyone kill the young man?"

"Who was second in command before Oscar arrived?"

Sinclair's eyes widened. "How would this help Liam's case? Why would he want us to look bad before Aldorf?"

"It's not that he's after," Gavin said. "The opportunity presented itself for him to lash out at Torquil and me, while causing us to have trouble with Aldorf."

"Take him. He will be traveling to Aldorf with us.

We will present him to the duke to do with as he wishes."

"He could spout information we'd rather the duke not know. Agree to tell lies to spare himself."

"True." Gavin stalked back to the guardsmen. "I will ask this once," he called out to the group. "Which of you killed Aldorf's messenger?"

His flat gaze scanned the faces and chills traveled up Beatrice's arms.

"Speak now."

None of the guard moved. Liam's jaw clenched and he spat on the ground. "He killed himself. Cut his own throat. Why would you accuse us?"

Gavin walked to Liam. "You know very well he didn't do it."

Before the man could reply, Gavin sliced his sword across Liam's throat. The guard's eyes bulged and he wrapped his hand over the injury as if to stop the flow of blood before falling backward onto the ground.

"Let it be noted. I will not stand for any traitor amongst our ranks." Gavin looked down dispassionately at the dying man. His blood gushed into the ground as his mouth opened and closed as death claimed him.

Beatrice could not look away between Gavin's hardened face and the dying man. She clutched Grisilda's hand while gasping for air.

Her pale friend tugged at her. "Let us go inside. This is for the men to handle."

Twice she'd seen Gavin kill, both times swiftly with dispassion. That side of him seemed foreign. He was not the same man who made love to her so thoroughly and gently at times.

As leader, his role was weighty. She understood it more each day.

Although it was understandable, why the guard had to die, to kill someone so dispassionately, didn't fit the same man who clung to her at night.

It stood to reason, there were many unsavory duties for a lord. Of course, she knew that. It was a wonder people would fight for titles and such. Although titles brought power and affluence, they were counterbalanced with a heavy yoke.

Her legs wobbled as she barely made it to the kitchens. Grisilda hurried to the stove to boil water. "We need some strong tea. Something to calm our nerves."

Molly neared. "What happened?"

"Two men are dead. Liam killed the messenger and

His Grace killed Liam," Grisilda explained to a gasping Molly.

"Lord help us." Molly crossed herself. "Why would Liam do such a thing?"

"He was angry that Torquil named Oscar as second in command." Beatrice placed her head in both hands, resting her elbows on the tabletop. "Torquil should not have done it. However, I wonder what type of leader Liam would have made."

"Precisely why he was not named," Molly said. "Torquil knows those men inside and out."

Grisilda let out a breath. "Nonetheless. We should pray for his soul." The women sat around the table as the water boiled and prayed. Beatrice also prayed that when the men went to Aldorf with the news, they would be safe and not end up dead as well.

"Now let's have some tea and wait. Once Liam's wife is informed, we'll have to ensure she and the young are taken care of."

"He was married then?" Beatrice's eyes filled with tears. "Oh no."

# CHAPTER FOURTEEN

C ASTLE CANAAN WAS on the road from Carlisle, where Gavin lived and Kendal in Cumbria. They were informed that De Wolfe lived there for the time being. Once they arrived and the heavily fortified castle, they escorted in to the great hall, where Scott De Wolfe greeted them. Gavin and Torquil exchanged confused looks at the warrior's demeanor. He actually smiled several times during their meeting.

"Lady Avrielle has changed the man completely," Torquil murmured on their way back home.

"Aye tis a different man. I rather like the new De Wolfe. Having his support means Aldorf will lose any desire to attack us. For even his forces cannot stand against De Wolfe's army."

"And still I must go," Gavin said not at all looking forward to be apart from Beatrice.

Torquil chuckled. "And return with haste I am willing to bet."

IT WAS ALMOST ten days since Gavin and Torquil had gone, along with twenty guards. Although Beatrice knew very little of the Duke of Aldorf, it was enough to worry about what happened.

With each day that passed, she grew more and more anxious. "What will happen if Gavin doesn't return?" she asked a harried Molly who oversaw the other helper in the kitchen while dropping vegetables into a pot.

"I do not know, Milady. However, it would not be unheard of for you to marry Sinclair as he will take over the reins of lordship."

At the idea, Beatrice recoiled. "I certainly hope not. How could I?"

"If you are with child, it would be the best recourse. Think of it. The child, if male, will carry his father's title and need protection. Once of age, he will become duke."

Beatrice rushed to the doorway. "Gavin better well return. I have no desire to marry his brother."

A maid giggled until Molly sent her a warning look. "I understand. But that is how things are done. Worry not. I'm sure His Grace will return any day now."

THAT NIGHT, BEATRICE lay in the dark unable to sleep. It was cold in the room as the fire had dwindled. Without Gavin next to her to share warmth with, it was hard to stay warm. Yes, the bedding was thick and she burrowed deeper into the covers, however, it didn't seem enough.

She looked to the fireplace where Lasitor had taken to sleeping since Gavin left. He had refused to take the hound with him.

A commotion rang out and Beatrice sat up. "Could it be?" At once fear coursed through her. Racing to the window, she peered down and could make out the men on horseback arriving into the inner courtyard. She could not make out in the darkness whether or not her husband was among them.

She backed away, grabbed her robe and raced out barefoot. At the stairwell, she slowed just enough to get her bearings in the dim light then scurried down to the great room.

The doors opened and she could hear the din of a conversation. "I need to bathe. However, it will have to wait until morning."

"Gavin!" Beatrice ran to him and threw herself into his open arms. "You returned."

"I'll take my leave," Torquil said with a chuckle. "Good night."

The feel of his body, the fact he stood upright and seemed unhurt, brought Beatrice to tears. "It—it took so long," she stuttered.

He wrapped his arms around her. Although she had to turn her head for he smelled of dirt and horse, a grin split her face. "I missed you as well, Beatrice." He pressed a soft kiss to her temple. "However, I cannot join you in bed. I am far too dirty."

"I'll help you bathe then." She tugged his hand and turned toward the kitchen. "Come. I refuse to spend another night alone."

Two sleepy lads were awakened and hurried to heat water and bring out the tub for Gavin. He promised them a day without tasks for their trouble. Neither seemed to mind as they chatted to him about what happened during his absence.

Finally, Beatrice oversaw his washing. She soaped his hair and rinsed it while hiding a smile when her husband's eyes drooped with weariness.

Once he finished his bath, they walked up the stairs to their chamber. He added a log to the fire and stoked it until it burned bright, then slid into bed next to her.

Gavin let out a sigh and yawned. "Any talk will have to wait until tomorrow."

Within moments, he fell asleep and so did Beatrice, happily snuggled next to him.

SHE WOKE TO kisses and Gavin over her, his mouth moving from her jawline down to her throat. Before long, they were a tangle of limbs as they sought the intimacy of lovers who'd been apart too long.

Their lovemaking was urgent and fast-paced, neither seeming to get close enough to convey how much they needed the intimacy they'd missed. Beatrice ran her hands down Gavin's back and cupped his bottom, pulling him closer while he thrust in and out of her, his body instinctively knowing what she needed.

It was a long time later that they lay spent. Beatrice sprawled over her husband, a lazy curve to her lips as she traced circles on his chest. "I believe I love you, Gavin."

His deep chuckle echoed in her ear. "I'm not surprised. You have to love me."

"What?" She pushed up and glowered down at him. "I don't."

"Yes. You. Do." He said each word between kisses.

"I don't wish to be the only one in love in this marriage. So I hoped you would."

"You love me as well?"

"I have since that day you helped me find my hound."

"Liar." Beatrice laughed, enjoying his mirth when he chuckled as well.

He wrapped his arms around her and pressed his cheek to her temple. "Perhaps it was when you almost shot me in the head with an arrow or when you accosted me in the garden at my uncle's keep."

"I did no such thing. It was you who attacked me." Beatrice kissed his jaw.

"No…no, if I remember correctly, you clung to me like a vine."

"I feared falling since you were leaning me backward."

They continued the verbal sparring, not noticing a red-faced Grisilda backing out of the room with a soft smile.

*Six weeks later.*

AT THE MORNING meal, Beatrice walked to the high

board and sat next to Gavin. He was deep in conversation with Oscar. One of Molly's helpers hurried over with a plate and placed it before her.

Beatrice blanched when her stomach revolted. After a few steady breaths, she was able to sip tea, but each time she looked to the food, the urge to vomit became worse.

"What's wrong?" Gavin studied her. Perspiration at the nausea coated her face.

"I don't feel well. I will go to Molly and ask for some herbs." She got to her feet unsteadily and managed to get to the kitchen before hurrying past it to throw up just beyond the doorway.

"I wondered if you were with child. All those late mornings since His Grace arrived had to produce something." Molly spoke from the doorway. "Now, hold steady for a moment. I will bring water for you to rinse your mouth with. Then some dry bread to steady your stomach…" the woman kept talking the entire time as Beatrice grappled with the news.

Why had she not kept track. Of course, since before Gavin left she'd yet to have her courses. By her calculations, she'd not had her courses since arriving there.

AND SO, IT was that in the next three years, Gavin Alexander Tavish Mereworth, Duke of Selkirk, and his wife, Beatrice Preston Mereworth, were blessed with two sons and a wee daughter they named Marybeth.

Soon after the wee girl was born, Beatrice drank a bitterroot tea regularly to keep her husband's seed from taking root. Three young were enough and she wanted to enjoy her husband and the young ones without fear of becoming continuously heavy with child as she and Gavin enjoyed making love often.

IT WAS A wonderful, sunny afternoon. Both Beatrice and Gavin spent time outdoors with the children. Beatrice chuckled when her husband reluctantly allowed the nursemaid to take the two lads to rest before the evening meal. The second maid waited until Beatrice finished nursing and took the four-month-old Marybeth.

"I have something planned I think you will enjoy." Gavin leaned forward and kissed her. "Change into clothing you can ride in. I'll go see about the horses."

Excited at the prospect of riding, she dashed around him and up the stairwell to their chamber.

Moments later, they rode with Oscar and two

guards behind. Beatrice noted they were all armed with bows and arrows and for the first time in a long time, her hands itched to hold her own.

"Where are we going?" she asked Gavin. He grinned at her then unfastened his bow from the horse's saddle. Along with it was hers.

"We, dear wife, are going hunting."

No sooner had he handed her the quiver and bow did she spur the horse to a gallop. Laughing as her hair came loose from its pinnings and flew around her head.

"I will best you, husband," Beatrice called over her shoulder.

Oscar laughed and looked to Gavin. "She will never be tamed you know."

"Aye," Gavin replied and shook his head. "I married the fiery woman and would not change anything about her."

As they gave chase, Gavin called out to her, "Wife, wait for us."

THE END.

Printed in Great Britain
by Amazon

29098343R00106